Angelo

The Dancing Imps of the Wine

Or, Stories and Fables

Angelo

The Dancing Imps of the Wine
Or, Stories and Fables

ISBN/EAN: 9783744786775

Printed in Europe, USA, Canada, Australia, Japan

Cover: Foto ©Andreas Hilbeck / pixelio.de

More available books at **www.hansebooks.com**

THE

DANCING IMPS OF THE WINE;

OR,

STORIES AND FABLES,

BY

ANGELO.

NEW YORK:
HURST & CO., PUBLISHERS,
122 NASSAU STREET,
1880.

PREFACE.

These Stories and Fables may read as if they sprang into existence as lightly and naturally as the Flowers of the Garden or the Fruits of the Orchard. But they are the result of deep thought, and of a close survey of the motives and actions of men, women, and children. Often when a superficial reader will but see, as it were, the calm, heaven-reflecting sea, the patient searcher after truths will discover in the ocean's depths vast forests of beautiful marine plants, beneath whose waving branches lie paths beautified by pink and white coral, variegated weeds, and ever-murmuring shells.

Like the Greek Philosopher, all the writer asks of his critics is to "Strike, but hear!" —satisfied to rest his claims to fame on the unbiassed, unpurchasable verdict of a great, free people, whose second sober thought is always right.

ANGELO.

CONTENTS.

PART I.—STORIES.

PART II.—FABLES.

THE
DANCING IMPS OF THE WINE.

A DREAM.

A STORY TOLD BY A GRANDFATHER TO HIS CHILDREN.

IN my younger days, drinking was more common than it is now. It was the custom, then, always to place liquor on the dinner-table.

One evening I had been drinking some sparkling wine; and the fumes getting into my brain, I fell asleep.

Suddenly I heard little feet pattering upon the table; and the most musical laughter resounded through the room. It sounded like the tinkling of glassy crystals.

Opening my eyes half stupidly, I saw the queerest vision. Little sparkling imps were dancing all around me on the table.

"Hello!" said I. "Who are you, and whence do you come?"

"Oh!" replied a little imp, with a chuckle, "don't you know?—you old ignoramus, you lazy old fool, you fuddled old nightcap!"

"No!" said I.

"Well, then, we'll enlighten you; we'll put some knowledge into your crazy old head.

"We are the IMPS OF THE WINE. We have been corked in, and imprisoned this many a year, in yonder old black bottle.

"But *you* have uncorked us, and given us freedom; and now we have expanded to our natural size. You saw us, but a few moments ago, dancing up and down in the wine you drank, like sparkling air-bubbles.

"Some of us have got into your head, and made you tipsy. Some have got into your heart, and made you feel young again. Some are tickling your brain with all sorts of queer fancies. Some will get into your feet, and hold you captive, so that you will reel and stagger as you try to walk."

I gazed at them in amazement, as they twisted and twirled and tumbled and jumped and danced and dodged,—seeming so light and airy.

Soon they became uproarious, and shouted and screamed in their merry glee. One got in each ear, and sang a gay song. Another climbed up in my nose, and danced a hornpipe there. Some got on my head, and leaped and scratched in my hair. Others jumped into my whiskers, and, hanging there, swung back and forth, chattering merrily.

They crept up my arm, and began to tickle me. They crept down my back, stroking it gently with their little glistening nails, until they almost set me crazy.

They played hide-and-seek through my clothing. At last my whole body was alive with these little frolicsome imps.

"You rascals!" I screamed; "get off, and away with you!"

They opened their little mouths, showing little shining diamond-like teeth, and laughed in derision; then suddenly stooped down, and pointed their tiny fingers to the wall.

'Twas covered with portraits and other paintings. A dog in one sprang from his place,— began to bow-wow, to dance on his hind legs, and caper with wild delight.

A tree in another picture moved out, and, standing in the center of the room, began to shake its leaves.

A horse in another leaped down, and began to trot around the room,—neighing loudly, snuffing the air in proud disdain, and prancing wildly.

Said I, "The room is bewitched." And all

the imps nodded and laughed gleefully, tapping me with their tiny fingers; and, in mockery, even poking them into my very eyes.

Some faces in a picture opened their eyes and winked at me. They rolled their heads out of the frames and saluted me. One even opened his mouth and laughed.

A lovely black-eyed witch in another kissed her hand to me, and shook her raven curls.

In another, there was a peasant fishing with a long rod. Suddenly he swung it around, and gave me such a whacking thump with it, that it made my ears ring; and the little imps screamed "Ha! ha! served you right!" and all the pictures shouted, in chorus, "Ha! ha!"

I looked on the floor. Was I dreaming? The chairs and tables seemed to have legs and feet. They began to waltz; and queer little heads peeped out of their tops, all covered with thick matted hair,—of white and red, black and yellow.

They arranged themselves in line, and, dashing at each other, pulled each other's hair out by handfulls, until the room seemed filled with feathers from the floating hair. Then they disappeared; and the carpet had all kinds of flowers, in beautiful wreaths, upon it.

These began to rise on tall green stems, to put out little shoots and branches, in which little buds began to grow and expand, until the whole room was full of perfume.

The wall-paper was all striped up and down, and the stripes seemed to start out; and, like snapping whips flying around me, cracked their snappers into my very face. Then they twisted themselves around my legs, like so many coiling snakes.

One picture was full of chickens, ducks, and geese. All at once they flew out; and, running around on the floor, began to cackle, and crow, and hiss, till the noise around me was terrific.

A green snake, coiled up in one corner of the picture, began slowly to unwind; and, darting out his tongue and elongating himself, hissed into my very ear.

In another corner was a bee, which began to fly about, and kept buzzing around my head,— lighting at last on my nose, and stung me.

I half arose with the pain, when, all at once, the imps shouted and leered at me furiously; and, with their little feet kicked me in the sides, scratched my head, pulled my nose, and tugged at my hair and whiskers.

Then one imp,—larger, wilder, and more wicked than the rest,—suddenly gave a loud whistle, and all in the room began to thump and beat me.

The horse kicked me on the shin; the dog got hold of my leg; the chickens and geese picked at my face with their bills; the tables and chairs leaped into the air, and punched me in the head; the tree fell over on me, and broke my leg; the fisherman hooked me in the eye; the snake crawled round and round my waist, hissing into my ears, looking into my eyes, and kissing my lips with its darting fangs; the bee lit in the other eye, half putting it out; while the young girl pulled my nose, and all the little imps kicked at me incessantly,—the whips from the wall meanwhile slashing continually.

I tell you I was frightened. I tried to start up, but could not. My ears were stunned with the noise, and I almost went mad with the pain. Again I started up, and I thought the horse gave me a terrible kick in the back, which made me leap in agony;—when, lo! I saw an old neighbor before me, who, just coming in, had given me a slap on the back, crying, "What! ho! neighbor! has the wine got the best of you? Why, you were fairly half-seas over!" And he laughed at my dismay.

I tell you I could hardly believe my deliverance was real; and the dream so impressed me, that, from that hour I forswore wine, and all its dancing imps.

From that day I have never tasted it; and, my children, it will be well for you to follow my example; or else the imps may get into your head, and torture you as they did me;—perhaps lead you into crime, even into murder, and so doom you forever.

THE SILVER FAIRY.

GROUP of merry children, of both sexes, were wandering in the woods, when, all of a sudden, a shower of nuts came raining down upon them.

Surprised, they looked up, and saw the queerest tiny object perched upon the branches. Frightened, they were about to run away, when the softest, sweetest voice, ever heard, told them to stay, and she would come down.

"My little friends," she said, "I am the Fairy of these woods."

She had little silver wings to her sides, a robe of silver spangles around her, and a beautiful silver wand in her hand, whose point was tipped with a tiny redbird's head; and, instead of eyes, were two lovely shining pearls.

On her head she wore a silver crown, soft and open as if lace,—its points all glittering with flashing diamonds. Her eyes were heavenly blue, large and radiant in light; and her soft silky hair, in curling tresses, shone like the whitest flax.

She shook her wand, and the air was filled with silver snow. She tapped the trunk of the tree with her wand, and it opened, showing a hole within; and out leaped a pair of snow-white reindeers, with silver bells and harness; and also a beautiful tiny sleigh, all of frosted silver, and full of sparkling radiance.

The robes were very thick and soft, and pure white. The reins were of silver cord; and the lining, cushion, and carpet of the sleigh, were made of silver cloth.

"Come!" said the Fairy, "who is a good girl? Who is a good boy? Who go to school regularly, obey their parents, and are kind to their brothers, sisters, and their little pets?   Who are polite to strangers, and courteous to all?"

All stood silent!

"What! are none of you good?"

Up started a little black-headed witch, with bold, blazing, dark, bright eyes, and said,—

"My brother is good!"

"Is he? Then enter, boy. What is his name?"

"Freddy."

"Well, Freddy! jump in, and take a glorious ride."

"Sissy is good!" said a little urchin.

"Well! what is her name?"

"Katy."

"Well, Katy! go in, too."

So, one after another, attracted by the lovely sleigh, and the pretty reindeers, all were found to be good, at last!   And all went in.

Round and round, through the trees, whirling and whirling, they kept on, till at last, descending a great hill, the sleigh flew over, and they all laughed in glee; but no one was hurt.

So, on and on, again they rode up and up the mountain side, till at last they reached the summit.

On the summit was a fairy's silver castle. The sun shone on it so beautifully, and its walls were so polished, you could see your face in it like a mirror.

The castle was full of silver turrets; and queer little silver images were sitting on each turret, with silver horns in their mouths, playing most delightful melody.

As they entered the castle-doors, these horns all at once blew a terrible blast,—so loud that the castle shook.

Then a band of spirits, all dressed in silver lace, light and gauzy, came forth and led us within.

The walls were of silver, decorated with beautiful flowers, leaves, and trees, engraved thereon,

—with silver wreaths in graceful foldings all around them,—strikingly beautiful.

The floors were raised up like a network of silver, in superb diamond patterns, and ornamental work.

The chairs were of the same metal, looking like strange images perched on carved legs, very beautiful.

Silver lounges, made like a wreath of wings all entwined together, marvelously beautiful and curious, and matted with snow-white down, were placed around the room.

Lovely pictures graced the walls, adorned with exquisite silver frames of the rarest workmanship and most ornamental patterns.

Gauzy curtains of silver fleece hung down from the windows, like curling clouds rolling o'er and o'er each other.

"I suppose you wonder, my children, you see so much silver!   But in these woods and mountains are vast mines, and I am Goddess of the ore. So silver is the symbol of my rank."

In the green pastures were beautiful snow-white horses and cattle, sheep, and hogs, in droves,—all as white as the driven snow.

In the stables, around the castle, silver harness in many a curious pattern was hung up, with fairy-like exquisitely ornamented silver phaetons on the floors.

The tables, all of solid silver, covered with silver, damask, and napkins, adorned the room.

The dishes, knives, and forks, and every utensil used, were of the same metal, chased and engraved in fanciful devices.

The servants were all dressed in tissues, like floating down, of the same ore; and it was a wondrous glittering sight, when the sun shone on all this splendor.

Suddenly a great giant, like a mighty metal statue, all studded o'er with glittering white diamonds, blew a great silver trumpet, sending forth a silvery peal; and, as if by magic, the great table in the center of the hall was loaded with the most delicious fruits and nuts.

The Fairy bade us sit down and eat. Such delicious melons, juicy grapes, such downy peaches, apricots, and nectarines, such sweet oranges, were never seen before.

They ate and ate till they could eat no more.

"Who," said the Fairy, "is the best child amongst you all?"

No one answered!

"Come! I'll give you little bits of silver paper, and lend you little silver pencils. Then you can write, with some of my silver ink, the name of him or her you think the best."

Instinct is wonderful! For all, without exception, wrote the names of Katy and Fred.

"Come here, my little dears!" And she placed a chain around Katy's neck, with a tiny watch attached, and a lovely ring upon her finger, and a rich bracelet on her wrist,—all of most beautiful silver patterns.

To Freddy she gave a pair of skates, a knife, and a hammer,—all of the same ore, very beautiful. To the others she gave nothing.

So, you see, my children, the good in the end are always rewarded.

Then the doors suddenly opened, and a great band of musicians, all dressed in silver cloth, were seated on a silver throne, with silver instruments in their hands.

All at once they played such tunes it thrilled us through and through,—so gay, so joyous, so full of spirit.

Each little sprite took one of us by the hand, and whirled us round and round in the dance.

We seemed to dance as if on feathers,—as if we danced on air. More lively grew the music, till, as we spun round and round, all objects disappeared, and we seemed to be in a whirling air of silver, and the music sounded like a liquid buzzing.

The whole earth seemed of silver. It seemed as if God had suddenly thrown this metal veil o'er Creation,—everything looked so strangely beautiful.

Suddenly we were transported through the air, as if on wings, and alighted at the foot of the same tree; and a voice in the air said to us, "Be good little children, and you often can come to the silver castle, and enjoy its music, and the dance."

Then the Silver Fairy bid us all good day.

THE
SKELETON ON THE WALL.

A DREAM.

"OH, tell us a strange dream!" said all the grandchildren, "do!" So the old gentleman gratified their wishes.

"A lady told me this story, and said it was a true one. It is called 'SKELETON ON THE WALL.'

"I dreamed I was staying at my sister's house; and in the bedroom was a stove near the wall, lighted with a coal fire.

"I slept; and suddenly I saw the wall open near the stove, which gave a misty light around the room; and a gaunt, weird skeleton, moved slowly out, having a strange fleshy hue in the soft glow of this half-smouldering fire.

"It solemnly, slowly advanced to my bed-side, with its long bony arm and hand extended toward me. Reaching my bed, it stopped, and holding its arm o'er my head, and gazing fixedly with an awful glare into my very eyes, solemnly pronounced these words: "*Come with me! your time is up!*" and thrice waved its arm o'er me; and then, with a strange gleam in its stony eyes, pointed its long fleshless arm on high.

"I saw on its bony finger outstretched, a signet emerald, very curious. I thought it an evergreen gem,—a type of Immortality.

"Its arm fell slowly, solemnly, to its side, again. It stood a moment, and gazed at me, as if to impress me indelibly with its words, murmuring, '*Remember!*' Then turned and marched back again,—when the wall opened, and it disappeared.

"It made a wonderful impression on my mind; and a few weeks afterwards my sister's husband came home, sick and weary, from the South.

"He was placed in that same chamber, and in a short time died.

"At the funeral I remembered my dream; and as I gazed at his awful, thin, wasted, pale, marble form and face, it seemed as if the skeleton was there, and gazed out of his dead eyes, and his emaciated features. And there, sure enough, on his long, withered, bony finger, glittered an *emerald!*"

"Oh, Grandpa! that is an awful story. Tell us another fairy story."

"I'll try, my children, and do my best to please."

And he told this Christmas Story.

A CHRISTMAS STORY.

IME, Christmas Morn. On a very sunny day, beneath a porch fronting the South.

'Twas a Christmas Morn, so beautiful!—as if God had sent down His sweetest light upon the earth. The snow lay upon the ground in feathery masses, while diamonds glittered on the trees, the shrubbery, and every object around.

'Twas almost a fairy scene. That neat old farm house, with its green blinds, and snow white paint; its roomy porch, surrounded with huge towering evergreens, while here and there

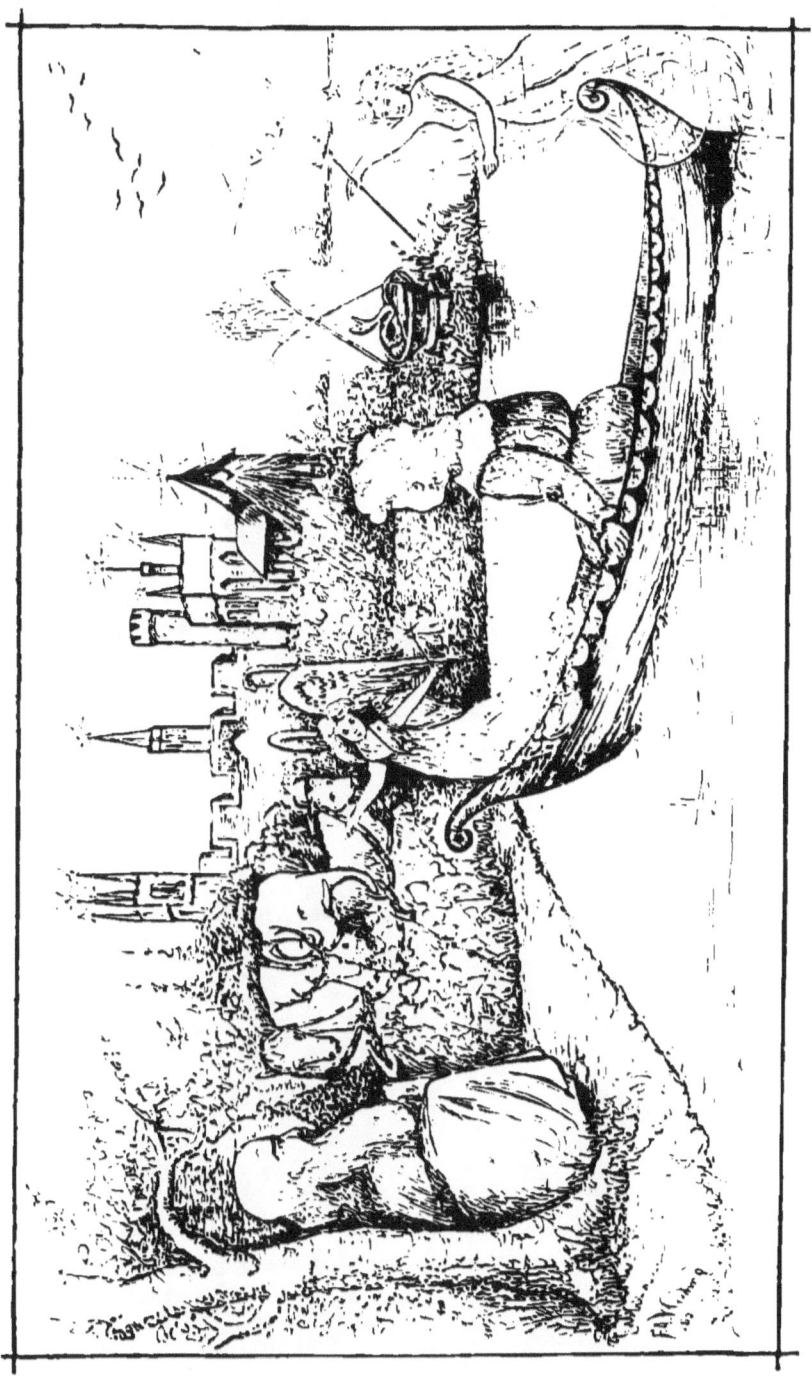

a stately oak loomed up to view, like an old giant, its great arms clasping the skies.

The house stood upon a sloping hill, bordering a sylvan lake, all frozen like a sheen of glass. The sun arose on that rural scene in a pure lustrous gold.

'Twas a heavenly light reflecting on that happy home, and lighting up such a group of merry faces.

On the porch, enjoying the sunny air, sat an aged woman, wrapped in furs. Her rich silver tresses hung down from beneath her snowy linen cap, and such a face! Almost as fair, with its soft flush, as that of childhood,—a face that belonged to a pure and happy life,—a good sweet face, full of pensive loveliness, and a kindly smile.

"Ah, Ganny!" said a lovely urchin only four years old, his dark dreamy eyes and fair rosy face almost concealed beneath a wealth of golden tresses, that looked like the sunbeams, in their rich and silky glow. "Ah, Ganny! do tell some puty 'tory." And with a kiss from his rosebud mouth, he coaxed the old lady to amuse him.

"Yes, yes!" all chimed in, "do tell!"

Ah! 'twas a sight of glory to see those eager young faces, all aglow, lit up with pleasure,—all intent to listen; their youthful fancies on tiptoe with expectation,—the dark brunette, the fair blonde,—some tall and stately; some stout and portly; some sad and musing; some wild, gay, and prattling,—of all sizes and ages,—watching their grandma's face to hear her speak, their eyes sparkling with glee.

Some came up and crouched at her knee; others put their little hands upon her shoulders. The little urchin climbed into her lap,—while some stood rapt, and gazed into her eyes; and one even left the porch and stood beneath the open sky.

A stillness like death fell on all around, while the grandma thus spoke:—

"My children, I well remember many and many a long year ago,—for now I am seventy, as you all know,—when I was a child, twelve years old, I had a dream, and such a dream! So strange and odd!"

"Yes! yes!" all replied, with eager delight.

"Do! do! Ganny!" said little four-year-old. And he shook his golden curls, clapped his hands in merry glee, and laughed aloud.

"At that age, I was full of strange fancies, for I used to read many Christmas stories, full of fables, fairy sprites, and dancing imps. That afternoon I read such a story; and when I went to bed, my little head was bewildered.

"It seemed as if fairies were all around me, and imps were dancing in my brain; and I could hear the sprites whisper in my ears, and strange antics were playing all around me.

"It seemed as if I was bewitched; and my little head, full of these follies, kept spinning round and round, till at last, weary, I slept;

but 'twas a broken sleep. I would turn over in restlessness, sometimes; then I started up in affright. Again, I spoke and laughed in my slumber. I was half conscious of some unusual stir in my chamber and in my brain;—and such a dream!

"I thought I was sailing upon a large river. The boat seemed of blue, like the sky, with a sail of gold. 'Twas a long, slim, fairy kind of boat, pointed at each end, and with jewels at the tips.

"The wind was laden with the perfumes of roses, and it all seemed dim and shadowy like, with a strange kind of purple light all around me.

"A being like an angel stood at the prow, with outstretched wings and hands pointing to the shore. At the helm stood a shadowy figure, almost a spectre in its dim outline.

"The boat glided on, its every motion like the breathings of a harp, till all of a sudden it stopped in the middle of the stream; and such a flood of light rushed upon me, as if all the stars were there gazing at me, and the queerest, yet most delicious music ever heard, burst upon my ears; and before me was a sight never to be forgotten.

"They were all dancing before an old man with long snow-white beard and curling locks, with a golden crown upon his head, and a crimson robe in many folds around his body. His eyes were blue like the heavens, and his face glowed like the dawn. His arms were folded, and he looked like a majestic statue of repose.

"It seemed as if all earth was there. Behind the old man arose in wondrous beauty and glittering transparency, a crystal palace with gleaming spires, like a vast jewel in the sun, reflecting all around million-colored hues of indescribable splendor.

"Fountains were playing before it, sending up many-colored waters of most delicious perfumes. Now, a shower of silver fell in sparkling streams with the sound of little tinkling bells; now 'twas of azure spray,—then it seemed all emerald, and again of shining gold; and where they fell into a crystal basin, every tiny drop changed into dancing imps, who gamboled and tumbled o'er and o'er each other, flinging upon the air tiny jets of foam, that gleamed like diamonds in the sun.

"In that brilliant light they looked like liquid fireworks in incessant play, yet far more wonderful; and as all this spray dropped gracefully in perpetual motion, it shone like colored jewels dancing in the air.

"Around every spire of this fairy structure, a revolving star shot forth sparks of colored fires, and fell around like shining snow. The whole air was thick with those dancing lights.

"Around the palace were all the flowers that ever grew, and seemed all alive with peering eyes, tiny little hands and feet. Some shook their leaves at me; some oped their petals as if about to speak; some nodded and winked; some cast their perfumes into my very nose in merry glee;—while others tumbled o'er and o'er, scattering their leaves upon the air.

"There was a smile and a laugh upon every flower. Some seemed to sing; some to hum; others to whistle; and queer little figures would rise from the petals, and dance and whirl on their tops, and bow their heads to me.

"Oh, 'twas a queer sight! and the whole air was buzzing with these strange sounds. The boat glided to the shore, and the old man beckoning us to approach, the angel took me by the hand, and led me to him.

"He laid his hand upon my head, as if to bless me. For a moment I stood bewildered, as though in a dream; and then, in childish curiosity, I asked him who he was.

"What! little beauty, do you not know me? I am called ENJOYMENT! Some name me

Pleasure! Others call me Jollity! I am Santa-Claus' prime minister."

"And sure enough, on a throne behind him little Santa-Claus sat in state, grinning from ear to ear; and reclining upon tiger robes, half asleep, at his feet, were a pair of the tiniest and most wonderfully beautiful snow-white reindeers,—while scattered near the throne were all the gifts of the Fairies to good little children, such as silver trumpets, little dancing-jacks, squeaking dolls, false faces of negroes and Indians, Chinese and Turks, little hobby-horses, little wooden farms and menageries, and all those things that delight little children.

"'Behold!' said the old Patriarch, 'my kingdom approach, my right royal subjects!'

"On came marching troops of animals, such as lions, tigers, wolves, camels, lambs, rhinoceroses, &c., all decked with parti-colored ribbons, that waved from head to head, and wound around their bodies.

"They danced and leaped in sportive glee, as if happy and grateful for another Christmas.

"Then came, tumbling o'er and o'er each other, long Tribes of Fishes,—from ocean, sea, lake, river, and stream,—dressed in gold and silver spangles, ever throwing from their mouths many-colored waters, that fell upon the air in perfumed spray.

"There were dolphins and mermaids, sunfish, starfish, and swordfish,—horseshoes, cuttle-fish, and flying-fish,—whales, porpoises, sharks, &c., —with old Neptune at their head, holding aloft his trident.

"They were full of frolic and merry antics, and rolled over and under each other continually, leaving their scales behind, that made the path look like a long line of gold and silver.

"After this, all the Insect Tribe appeared: queer bugs and worms, fantastically striped snakes, coiling in queer fashion round and round each other.

"These sent up a mighty buzz, a prolonged hiss, a strange rattle, filling the air with the oddest sounds possible.

"The Butterflies, in innumerable battalions, fairly darkening the air, like a swinging cloud, came floating around the old man's form.

"Some crept into his whiskers,—others nestled in his curling locks. Again, some toyed with his eyebrows; others hid within the folds of his long robe. One even fluttered upon his lips, and there hummed his blithesome song. They were beautiful as sailing rainbows,—all light and radiance.

"All the Birds of the Air breathed forth their souls in music as they came winging on, flock after flock, all joy and carol,—light and cheery as a zephyr. There were cooing doves, robin redbreasts, bobolinks, soft-voiced nightingales, little wrens, whippoorwills, golden canaries, gold and silver pheasants, bobwhites, witching magpies, chattering parrots, enchanting mocking-birds,—all filling the air with a paradise of sweet songs,—a living glory to all around.

"The Fruits then passed on, with their little round bodies stuck on two pipestem legs; and little eyes all around them, and mouths all over their bodies.

"They kept continually rolling their eyes at me as they marched, grinning and opening their mouths, as they danced and leaped fantastically.

"They seemed to have voices; for one said, 'How pale he is!'—referring to a white peach. 'Oh, my! how yellow!'—gazing at a young lemon. 'Look! is he not red-faced?'—pointing to a blushing apple. 'How purple!'—looking at a right royal grape. 'Ah! how she blushes!'—examining a luscious peach. 'The down is just growing,—only a fledging!'—

directing the attention to some young fruit. Thus they mocked each other, in frolicsome glee.

"There were whole orchards of golden pears, purple plums, wax-like grapes, downy peaches, blushing apples, luscious melons, perfumed oranges, juicy pine-apples, tamarinds, dates, and bananas,—all moving so nice and sweet, as if ready to drop into your mouth.

"Then came—of all sights the funniest ever seen—all the eggs that were ever laid by bird, or insect, or reptile, marching on.

"They had little stems for necks, and two pipestem legs with red trousers on, and red buskins on their feet. Their little heads were covered with mops of hair,—some green, some blue, some white, some red, some yellow,—and their little heads kept continually bobbing up and down, and sometimes they entirely hid within their shells.

"They took long strides, and gave themselves

all kinds of airs; and kept their shells far in-
clined backwards, proud as so many walking
peacocks.

"Sometimes they ran all together, and you
could hear the little shells crack like the snap
of a whip; and then they set up such a screech
it made my ears tingle! Each egg had a little
pipe in its mouth, and all kinds of colored
smoke curled up in tiny cloudlets, very beautiful.

"In front, as a leader, came a big ostrich-egg,
with a big ostrich-feather on its top, and a
dozen such stuck all around its sides. It seemed
almost concealed in feathers; and it kept dancing continually, and seemed like a waving of
plumes.

"But a stranger sight than this marched behind. 'Twas all the Feathers that ever grew,—
one after another, like an array of plumes;
and as they bent and swayed in the breeze,

it made a mighty rustling as if of wings, and each feather whirled round and round.

"At times they filled the air with soft breezes, indescribably delicious. It fell upon my ear like a lullaby. These breezes were full of odd tunes of sweetest melody.

"Sometimes the air would carry one feather on top of another till they seemed to touch the sky,—then all at once dissolved, and came floating down, as if they were fancy plumes of snow.

"The last of this curious train were the Fairies and Sprites, Elves and Satyrs, Centaurs and Gnomes, Fauns and Wood-Nymphs, and Water-Sprites.

"They were loaded with blossoms, and decked in curious leaves; and all were playing curious instruments. A little fairy was ensconced in a buttercup, riding on the back of a huge centaur. A little sprite peeped out of a lily, on a satyr's back. A little gnome was half hid in some rose-leaves,—while some wood-nymphs were holding lovely bouquets, and a dozen elves were looking over the rims, and laughed at me.

"One lovely nymph had a strange troop of spiders in her train, her robes being all stuck over with them. They were formed into bouquets in her hair; and, while she walked on, they kept crawling all over her, making me shudder, as some were covered with moss, being big and ugly.

"All at once they stopped, and 'MERRY CHRISTMAS!' burst upon my ear.

"Overhead hung a great golden cloud. It opened; and a voice, sweeter than the song of the stars, spoke to the listening crowd.

"'I am NATURE! Behold my glory!—my people!—my treasures! I am God's servant, —to delight mankind, give them food and clothing, make them happy and content. God gives them music and dancing, beautiful insects, many-colored songsters, sparkling jewels and fountains, luscious fruits and grains, shining ores, many-veined marbles, variegated woods, lovely-hued flowers, delicious perfumes, parents and children,—and Christ as an atonement, who will lead them to Nature, and up to Nature's God,—who, far beyond this golden cloud, reigns in glory, ever waiting to crown you, like this old man, with a golden wreath, and bid you all A MERRY CHRISTMAS!'

"The cloud disappeared; and, as I looked around, all had vanished. Methought I stood alone upon the river's bank, when suddenly I awoke.

"'Twas morn; and 'MERRY CHRISTMAS!' fell upon my ear. I looked forth: there was the lake full before my view."

THE

FROG JUBILEE OF ANIMALS.

"TELL US," said a little, pretty, blue-eyed child, to his grandfather, "a funny story about animals."

I will try to please you.

There was to be a grand Frog Jubilee, one bright moonlight night, about midnight, when all the world was presumed to be asleep.

All the animals, insects, birds, and reptiles, were invited to show their grievances, trials, and sorrows.

There was a great old stump in the middle of the stream, and the frogs gathered on that in immense numbers,—while all the animals were to recline upon the shore in the soft green grass.

A tree, near by, would receive the birds and insects.

A big Bloody-Noun (a very large frog) was to be the orator of the evening, as well as presiding officer.

There was to be a great gathering of hens and chickens, a-cackling and a-crowing,—ducks a-quacking, geese a-hissing, dogs a-barking, horses a-neighing, asses a-braying, cows a-lowing, sheep a-baaing, cats a-mewing, birds a-whistling and singing, bees a-humming, pigs a-grunting, crickets a-chirping,—even worms, toads, and beetles, mosquitoes, and insects.

After all was silent, the Frog stood up on his hind legs, expanded himself to his full dignity, and thus addressed them:—

"My Friends: I thank you for this vast gathering of the *elite* of the tribes of the earth.

I thank you warmly for this brilliant assemblage of the glory of the Animal Creation.

"I see around me many beautiful songsters: the buzzing fly; the elegant, sylph-like mosquito; the gay, hopping grasshopper; the stout, sturdy beetle;—even the little, lowly, crawling worm.

"This, my friends, is not an aristocratic assemblage, but a truly democratic gathering, where the lowliest has as much right as the grandest to speak out his mind and feelings. Let us, then, give to the little worm the first right to speak."

They all, with one acclaim, shouted, "Amen!"

THE WORM

wriggled up on an old log in the grass, and opened its tiny mouth to speak.

"I am only a MITE, yet the good God made me; and I think—since He took the trouble to make me, and gave me food to eat, air to breathe, and sunlight to see,—I have as much right to live as man. But how am I treated?

He invents, out of old iron, a curling hook with a sharp point to it, and digs in the ground to find me. He then cruelly takes me in his great ugly fingers, and alive impales me on this hook. It runs through my vitals! He has no remorse!—no conscience!—but brutally makes me writhe, and groan, and squirm, in agony. This is not all. With me he deceives the poor little silver and gold scaly fishes. They think, poor things, they are going to have a nice dinner. Instead, they get their jaws cruelly pierced and torn by this awful hook, are driven from their beautiful liquid home, dragged on the hard earth, and then eaten by this savage monster, man!"

They all cried, "'Tis a shame!"

THE DOG

then gave a "bow-wow."

"My friend," said the FROG, "do you wish to speak?"

Another "bow-wow!" and the dog wagged

his tail, his eye sparkled, he shook his shaggy body, and stretched himself out, and holding up his head with great dignity, said:—

"Although I am often treated with great friendship by man,—often kept as a pet, and allowed to frolic with the children, which I return by my faithful watching of their homes, by my fidelity, and desire to please him,—yet often ugly boys throw sticks and clubs at me; and once they tied a tin kettle to my tail, and shouted so, and hooted me so much, and chased me with stones, till I was almost mad with running.

"Then a great ugly boy teased me, till I became furious, and bit him. He went crying to my master, and lied about me.

"My master, indignant, seized a club, and broke one of my legs. So you see, a poor dog has sometimes a hard time of it, even if he does not work.

"Yet sometimes they put me to churning,

and force me to go on till I am ready to drop down dead.

"I often drag their wagon, with my master's children in it.   I don't mind this much; but often they invite the neighbor's children in, too; and make me drag a load only fit for a horse.

"Is this right?—is this fair?"

"No! no!" they all cried.

"See how gentle I am!   They pull and haul me about in every fashion; and if I bite one of these annoyers, they cry at once, 'Mad dog! mad dog!' and, in their base cowardice, beat me unmercifully, till I die."

Just then, although late,

A FOX

from the neighboring mountains came limping along, tired and dust-stained.   They all arose, and saluted him.

"The Fox! the Fox!" and all gave him three cheers.

The Fox, you must know, was a very polite fellow, very cunning and artful, very smooth and polished, and insinuated himself into their good graces with his beauty, his elegance, and his *bonhomie.*

He was smart, too, and knowing,—a kind of bookworm among the animals,—given to study and tricks,—a kind of natural conjurer, adroit and sharp-witted,—very fond of *grapes* and *chickens!*

He looked around at some *fowl* near, as if he longed to take a bite; and no doubt would have made them *fare*, if this had not been a peace-meeting, and universal amity had not been declared. If he had dared to break the law, all the animals would have killed him.

They all, with great politeness, invited him to speak, as his home was quite far away.

So he spruced up his fur, to look right genteel, and thus spoke:—

"My very dear, sweet, kind friends: I return

with very great love—especially for *chickens* (and there was a furtive gleam in his cunning eye)—your warm welcome; and I hope hereafter to reciprocate this noble reception (looking out of the corner of his eye languishingly at a fat duck near).

"My sorrows are many. Why, even last night, as I was about to dine on a fat hen,—I own it, friends!—here all the poultry edged away from him,—when, lo! I caught my foot in a brutal ugly trap, which the fiendish farmer made for me, and I lost a bit of my leg to get free. See here, for yourselves!

And he held up a leg which was bloody and sore. They all cried, "How mean!"

"This ugly man rode around the country next day, and told all the neighbors there was a Fox in his barnyard last night. He showed them all a piece of my leg.

"The scoundrel! the scoundrel!" they all cried.

"Then these big brutal men, on great beasts of horses, next day with great hunting-dogs, scoured the country to find me.

"They ran and shouted. The dogs ran and howled, as they smelt my track. Once they got a peep of me, but I dodged them round and round, and so got clear at last, or else I would not be here.

"Think of it! A great lot of booby men spending time and money, wearing out the horses, to catch a little thing like me! One hundred against one! Is it manly? Is it fair?

"No! no!" they all cried; "'tis cowardly!"

"So it is," said the Fox. "I agree with you. One or two got their deserts, any how; for one, in going over a fence, his horse stumbled, and the fool broke his leg on the top rail! I guess he'll remember me for some time, at least!" And he gaily chuckled, and licked the wound on his sore leg, as if the broken leg was a good salve for it.

"Then another got his horse in a deep hole, which threw him over his h'a', and broke the horse's neck in the struggle. There's two hundred dollars for a morning's sport!"

And again he chuckled! Then all the company stood up, and gave three groans for these ugly men.

THE MOSQUITO,

without waiting for any to ask him to get up, flew right on the stump beside the BLOODY-NOUN, and began to whiz.

The FROG looked surprised at this breach of etiquette.

"Oh, ho! Froggy!" And he tapped him on the shoulder, with a familiar air.

"I must be off; so I'll say a few words, and go. You see, I used to have a grand hunting-time with men, their wives, and babies.

"Game was always plentiful, when some

mean fellow invented nets, and covered all the doors and windows, so I can scarcely get a bite!

"So you see, my friends, by a base invention of man, by his selfishness, afraid of a few drops of blood,—like a pig, he wants all to himself!

At which all the pigs gave a sour, mad grunt!

"I have to sail the whole livelong night, to save myself from starving.

"This is why I want to speak, and fly off to get my supper. If by chance I do get in, they take napkins and slap the walls an hour before retiring, in order to kill me,—the bloody-minded monsters!

"They won't allow me even a sip! They are so ugly, they chase me around continually.

"I have to watch till they get asleep, and then I keep at the nets till I find a hole to enter.

"I'll be even with them yet; for I often

find some lazy boors asleep at their work, and then I dine like a king!"

With a flippant dip of his saucy head, he whistled a tune, and soared, on a light breeze just coming o'er them, serenely away.

Just then, the FROG, espying a

WATER-PILOT

climbing on the stump, invited him amongst them, and called upon him to speak.

"Oh, my friends, man hates me, and the dogs are death to me!

At this the dogs gave a sullen growl.

"I am despised by all, and why? Because I am so quiet, gliding, and noiseless. If any man is found base, traitorous, and mean,—lo! they call him a SNAKE!

"Burr, Arnold, and Grouchy betrayed their country!—they are SNAKES!

"My friends, I never betrayed my country! Why, then, should man liken me to these renegades? Why, then, should such be honored with my name?

"I am always true to my birth, my breeding, my nature, my instincts? I only want to live as God designed me to live, and I think it a shame for man thus to slander me.

"Why, even a big brute of a man shudders at my soft, sleek, oily figure, and runs away, or else he must get a stick to fight me!

"He is afraid of me; and yet my tongue is not half as bad as the tongue of a liar, the fangs of a slanderer, or the dart of a gossip!"

He ceased; and they all said he was too much abused!—much slandered!—and that many men,—aye, even women, too,—were not half as good as the honest SNAKE, who only wanted a living, with the powers he possessed to gain it.

The FROG, looking around, saw

A MONKEY

grinning with open mouth, scratching his head

with his feet, and his hand grabbing something very much like a louse or flea!

"Ah! my Darwinian manikin!—(see Fenni-more Cooper),—my wonderful little man!—what have you to say against your own relations?—this ugly man! You most truly resemble him,—and I should not wonder you was his four hundred and fifty-fifth cousin! —on the Devil's side!

"You carry, 'tis true, a long tail, instead of a walking-cane; and are rather more hairy, perhaps!

"Your phrenological developments are not so large! Still, on a dark night, when you stood on your hind legs, well dressed *a-la-mode*, in the fashion of the *elite*, you might well pass for a York dandy, or a high-bred exquisite!"

The Monkey grinned, turned a pirouette, scratched his head, pulled his tail, and leaped several times in the air, to show his agility. He is a gymnast, like man, you know, only a superior one. Then, with the most laughable and solemn gravity, as if he was a Demosthenes or a Cicero, a Butler or a Conkling, he began to stretch out his form to the uttermost,—so that he truly resembled some low orders of mankind.

"My very good, kind friends: I beg leave to say that I have no desire to resemble man in the least!—and I tell you why!

"I don't slander my fellow monkeys, as he does his kind; nor do I lie to gain possession of what don't belong to me!

"I do not hoard up large possessions, as he does, while so many are starving! When we have plenty, we freely divide among all our tribe. We are open and generous, and don't get drunk, like man, and make beasts of ourselves!

"We don't kill our wives and children, as men do! We are not quacks or public robbers!

—

"When we have enough, we are satisfied; but man is always hungering when he has more than enough!

"We don't hoard up, and deny ourselves the common necessaries of life, as man does!

"We are not such fools as he is! We don't steal ten dollars, and become slaves in a jail for years,—deprived of freedom, joy, and pleasure!

"We don't chew nasty weeds, and make ourselves disgusting to all nice folk! No, indeed!

"So, Mr. Frog, I am highly indignant at that fool Darwin, for his learned folly, to try to make us related! I despise the compliment! I consider it highly derogatory to our tribes to resemble man in anything!

"He is a poor tool, that man, any way you take him! He is always grumbling,—always dissatisfied!

"Why, even Adam and Eve, once, they say, had a Paradise, and, silly creatures! they got kicked out of it! They have not got any sense! They are always squabbling and fighting about their churches, the color of their skins, their ancestry and lineage!

"They always set themselves up continually, one above the others, and worship jewelry, dress, fashion, and money!

"See them continually changing their garments, and always looking at themselves in glasses!

"I am sick of their conceits!—their mummeries!—their follies!

"I consider it a shame for you, Mr. FROG, in any way or manner, to allow yourself to see any resemblance between my honest, manly, noble tribes, and this upstart, Man,—who claims descent after us!—so Darwin says, and he ought to know!"

All the company begged the FROG to make
an apology for this oversight, and soothe the
wounded pride of the MONKEY, by solemnly
declaring, at once and for all, that the monkey-
tribe considered itself always insulted by this
supposed resemblance!

The polite FROG said,—

"I see I have been misinformed; and I
assure you, I plainly see your infinite supe-
riority to that cowardly animal, Man,—who
has dared, through the great Darwin, to as-
sume this relationship, on his own respon-
sibility.

"I further will take a minute of this meeting,
by our secretary, Mr. FLY, who will supply
his own ink, and forward the same to Mr.
Darwin, who then will manfully, no doubt,
give his science a farther and a deeper study;
and do you, oh MONKEY, strict justice in the
future! Do you all agree to this?"

"Ay! ay!" all responded.

Then THE HOG
began to grunt,—he was getting hungry! The
Frog politely saw his condition, and allowed
him to speak.

He got up; and, giving another grunt, in
great self-satisfaction, began:—

"I am well fed,—that is, in amount,—but
the silly farmer throws all the refuse to me,
and keeps this refuse in a dirty swill-barrel,
which is never cleaned. So all the food I get
is sour and diseased!

"It is often kept in the sun, which makes
it smell! Then he expects me to be fit to eat!
He gives me more than I ought to eat, till I
get so fat, if I once get down I can't get up
again!

"So he ruins my liver and my digestion;
and I get awfully scabby and scrofulous, and
die. I often get queer little worms in me, and
poison the people.

"Who is to blame? Not I! I don't wonder the Jews are more sensible, wise, and good.

"They leave me alone; but other men make me a mass of disease, by allowing me to wallow continually in my own mire; and then they think me so sweet, they kill and eat me!

"But I will repay him by giving him various diseases from my body.

And he gave another grunt.

"It is like the water the great city drinks, —full of filth in the refuse of all the country's waste! The great city laughs at the country, and gets its old cast-away rubbish in its veins and blood!

"Oh, most wise city! Oh, great people! They spend millions on their backs, in their houses, in their jewels, and allow their stomachs to be diseased, and their veins poisoned! What think you, animals? Is this man so much, after all? Is he not a blind, silly fool? Has he any sense and judgment?"

"No! no!" said they all, at once.

Then a fat

HEN

cackling, our wide-awake FROG bid her go on. She said:—

"You see, all of you, how nice, sleek, and fat I am.

And she ruffled her feathers bravely.

"We do! we do!" they echoed.

"Well, you think I have a very nice time of it, no doubt.

"Man feeds me to the full, till I am in a fine state of *embonpoint*. Is it for our own good? Oh, no! Is it generosity? Oh, no! Is it a desire to make us happy? Oh, no!

"What then? To feed his huge belly,— which, like a leech, always cries for more! He stuffs me almost to bursting, in order to stuff himself!

"He takes away my children before my very eyes, and makes roasts of them!

"The wretch!" they all cried.

"And, as bad as the Spanish Inquisition, turns me on a spit before a hell-fire, and browns me like a nigger!"

They all sighed but the Fox, who was just about to return home. He gave a very prolonged sigh, and had half a mind to make a grab for her, but the country was too open.

Then the big black

BEETLE

began a drowsy hum; and the gentlemanly Frog, catching the dulcet notes, said:—

"Why, my friend, are you sleepy?"

"Yah! yah!" he muttered.

"Give us your experience," said Mr. Frog.

"I am tabooed by man; for everywhere he sees me, he puts his foot on me. If I get into his garden and spade it up for him, so that his vegetables may grow—half the time being too lazy to do it for himself—why, he scratches me out of the ground, and hits me with his spade."

"The horrid brute!" they all groaned.

A SHEEP

just then gave a great "Baah!" like a big baby crying, and the Frog nodded to him to proceed.

"My very good friends: I feel rather *sheepish* in this large company; especially as I have to follow so many distinguished strangers. Be patient for a few moments, till I tell my story.

"I have, you must know, a soft woolen cloak, which God gave me, to keep me warm. Well, envious man, thinking he knows more than God, meanly puts on his own back my robes; and then struts so vainly with it, like a human peacock!"

Then he gave a great "Baa!" They all joined in, and gave a great "Baa!" It was a

musical treat far superior to either Rubenstein
or Bulow, for it was more natural. It was
not learned or studied; so there was a genuine
magnetism about it far superior to any study.

Then a

CAT-BIRD,

like a flying negro, began to call like a CAT.
At first the FROG was nonplussed, and was just
about to cry "Pussy! Pussy!" when the bird
sailed over his head, and gave a gentle fanning
with his wings.

The FROG felt this soft flutter in the air,
and at once saw his mistake.

"Proceed, my young friend. We are all de-
lighted to listen to your dulcet voice,—a feathered Nilsson!—a flying Lind!—a full-fledged
Grisi!"

He then gave them a grand concerto in A
minor, a few trills, a few soft cadences, with a
prolonged dying wave of melody, and thus addressed them:—

"I am very useful to man, in various ways; but ugly boys continually point at me with their long, murderous guns. They steal our eggs; and keep great, horrid cats, to devour our little ones."

The CATS here set up a united "Meow!" and looked as if they would rush upon him.

"What wicked boys!" said they all.

Just then, a smooth, sleek, corn-fed

RAT

came tramping through the grass.

"Better late than never!" he gaily said; and bowed his head, gave a keen sharp glance around, and whisked his tail.

I tell you all the cats' mouths watered to have a bite of him! They kept up a soft meowing among themselves, as if the meeting was a stay upon their appetites.

"Oh, Mr. RAT," said our polite FROG, bowing his stately head; "we welcome you to this grand multitude. How is your health, and how are all the little MICE?"

"Oh, I left them nibbling in my lady's bureau; and I am in prime condition."

"Indeed, you have the free swing of the house; and you are thus a favored mortal."

"I don't know about that, Mr. FROG. I tell you, my provision business don't always pay; and 'tis often hard and dangerous work to accumulate stock enough for my grocery-store.

"You see, some evil men have invented so many curious traps, that puzzle us all. They are so very ingenious, so inviting, often so carefully concealed, or appear so innocent and harmless, that, in spite of our well-known caution, our sharp glances, our wide-awake senses, we are woefully humbugged!

"My brother last night lost his tail! My cousin the other day left his leg in a trap of steel springs! And only a few weeks ago my old father, who was too slow and half blind, got his neck broken in one of them, and we found him dead!

"Then they employ so many monstrous CATS ——

The CATS looked at him, black as a thundercloud, and spotted him, mentally determined to pounce upon him when the meeting was over.

"who chase us up and down; and, like sneaks, they watch for us, for hours,—sometimes stay near our holes almost a day, like LEECHES or SNAILS!

At these remarks, the CATS set up such a terrible caterwauling, and became so noisy, that all the animals shouted—

"Put them out! Put them out!"

This brought them to their senses.

"So you see, the freedom of the house and barn is full of danger. I have always to be on my guard, till I have become full of suspicion."

They all sympathized with the RAT very much, and thought his life a hard one.

A FLY

kept buzzing about the old FROG's head, as if impatient.

"Well, Mr. FLY, I see your little eye! So give us your life, before you die!"

"Oh, brutal man delights to destroy me!— his best scavenger, to eat up all impurities! Some mean grocer—no doubt to adulterate his dried currants!—invented a kind of paste spread on coarse paper, to catch me.

"I unconsciously alight on this, and stick fast; and there I linger, in great agony, till I die of hunger, and grief, and poison.

"Alas! alas!" they all cried.

"Then, again, they put some sweet water in a tumbler, and place a piece of bread over this, with a hole in it. I fall through, and get drowned. Are not these dirty tricks?"

"Oh, yes!" they all murmured.

Just then   A FLEA
a saucy FLEA, out of fun pinched the FROG's
ear.

He jumped up, as if about to dance the
polka, when the FLEA leaped before him.

"Oh, ho! my hop-of-my-thumb! Are you
there?"

"No!" said the FLEA; "I'm here, there, all
over, and no where!"

"Indeed, you are a real jack-o'-lantern!—a
true will-o'-the-wisp! What sorrows have
you?"

"Well, not many; but I get entangled in the
hair, sometimes; and men, and animals, and
birds, hunt me up, and crush me.

"After I have feathered my nest with so
much pains, it is awful to lose one's life
for it.

"Once a wild Italian stole a dozen of my
relations, and bribed them, by letting them
suck the blood of his arm; and so kept them

as captives, put tiny mites of silver collars around their necks, made them draw a train of cars along a track, pull up a bucket from a well, dance freely, and many other curious tricks. (True!)

"Well," they all cried, "you are generally lucky, and well able to take care of yourself."

He laughed, and struck a Horse on the nose, tumbled head over heels in a Monkey's ear, let fly a salute on a Sheep's back, and then danced on the breeze.

Then the Frog heard a soft low, like a dying moan, upon his ear; and then a poor rack-o'-bones of an old dilapidated

cow

came shambling up, a sight of pity to all. She was so weak she could hardly stand. Her tail was rotted off, one of her horns was gone, and great scabs stood all around her body.

A kind of rheum oozed out of her eyes, and she looked the picture of patient despair.

As the animals gazed at her, a terrible shudder shivered them with horror; and some even veiled their faces at the sight, while one pityingly murmured,—

"Can such things be?"

"Ah, Mr. FROG, let me tell you my life, so that the world can sympathize with my sorrows. You don't know how I am abused!—how miserably fed!—how kicked around!—standing weeks in filth!—and fed on hot, burning, nauseating swill!

"But I repay! Thousands of infants die yearly from my diseased milk! A howling wail goes over the land from the slaughter of the innocents!

"Even when I am a mass of diseased rottenness they milk me! And lo! the great cities—so dainty, so aristocratic, so great-minded,—whose refined noses turn up at the perfumes of poverty, yet sup in their morning coffee, their punches at noon, and their tea at eve, this watery slime,—little knowing, and apparently careless, they are planting seeds of disease that will take thousands of dollars to eradicate in the future!

"Oh, swill! great is thy throne! Oh, wealth! great is thy fraud!

"Oh, Mr. Frog, what think you of the law that is powerless to stop this diseased nuisance?

"What think you of the people who supinely permit this outrage?

"Good God! What are legislators for, when corruption fattens before their very eyes, and lo! they are blind and senseless!"

That poor old cow was a bitter satire on mankind!—a melancholy proof of the injustice, the stupidity, and the laziness of man!

All the animals gave a very prolonged groan, and turned up their noses in supreme disdain at man's folly and greed.

One indignant animal appealed to GOD, and besought Him to rain plagues on mankind,— make them a mass of disease! Let them suffer the tortures this poor Cow undergoes, till sense returns, and the filth of the stables is done away with forever!

The FROG suddenly felt a bite on his topknot, and softly put up a paw to catch the rascal.

"Oh, ho! my fine fellow! Have I got you? Why, you saucy

LOUSE!

And before all the animals he showed up the thief.

"What have you to say for yourself? Heigh ho! To think of such a visitor! Such a gay intruder! Such an exquisite!"

"Oh, Mr. FROG, I was so hungry at this protracted meeting, that I thought it was a Methodist love-feast, and so I thought I'd take a bite!

"You are so plump, full-fed, Mr. Frog, that you'll not mind it much, and 'tis truly a god-send for me!"

The kind, generous Frog, freely forgave him, and told him to freely expose his sorrows.

"I am only a Mite, but the world stares at me when I'm seen, as if I were a Monster! They make a great fuss always at my presence!

"Why, even the poets make fun of me; and bonny Burns addresses me as a Louse on a fine lady's bonnet!

"But you all know I generally keep my bed. In truth, I am almost always bed-ridden. Yet awful cruel man scalds me to death, pours boiling water into the holes, and burns me out.

"I do a little gardening on my own account in his scalp, and he makes a great pow-wow over it, and buys horrid rakes (combs) to scratch me out.

"Yet I love mankind! I am only social and friendly!

"I truly love this man, and sweetly press him with my soft lip! 'Tis my ardor that makes me press him so hotly!—my energy of passion!—my earnest embrace!

"Man can not sympathize with this free-love; but CLAFLIN and WOODHULL can, and all the rest of the masculine feminines!"

THE CAT

softly meowing, our noble FROG signed to her to speak.

"Oh, friends!" she said, in her gentlest, most purring tone, that fell upon the ear like down upon the air.

"I am quiet if they do not vex me,—if they don't rub the fur the wrong way; but if I take a frolic at night and have a grand **pow-wow**, you ought to see the sticks and brickbats a-flying!—old bottles, too!—all kinds of odds and ends!

"Can't I have a little fun, as well as man? Oh, no! They can make the night hideous with their sprees,—make fools of themselves all night long,—and this is all right!

"Turn about is fair play! Suppose we peppered him as he does us, how would he like it?"

All the animals said there was no fair play with man.

An old, battered, half blind, half lame, half dead, thin, angular, bony, worn-out

HORSE

gave a ghost of a neigh, which the gallant Frog hearing faintly, he directed his sympathetic glance that way, and was just about to invite him to speak, when the Horse had a terrible fit of wheezing and coughing. At last he stopped, and said:—

"Good friends: You see me as I am,—my looks alone tell the tale! I was misused, over-burdened, driven beyond my speed, half fed,

half littered, half sheltered, half groomed, getting more knocks than kindness; and so, before
my time, I look like this old battered hulk you
see before you.

"'Tis time to stop brutality, and learn man
mercy, gentleness, and forbearance,—time to
have found a true friend in BERGH!—a fearless
champion!—a brave and a humane man!—
who nobly does his duty without fear or favor!"

The HORSE had just spoken, when he fell
over dead.

It dampened the spirits of the assembly,
this sudden death, and all felt very sorry over
this much-abused and fallen champion of all
work.

All the animals with their feet and paws
dug a wide trench near a shady tree, and
buried him,—while many a moan filled the
solemn chambers of the night air.

Then a sudden, terrible roar, was heard,
which made all the animals tremble; and they

were about to flee away in terror, when a majestic

LION

leaped into their presence with another terrific roar that fairly shook the air, and seemed like muttering thunder.

He wildly shook his shaggy mane, gave three or four frantic leaps, lashed his tail fiercely, and seemed about to madden himself into a wonderful indignation.

How grand he looked! His yellow eye shone like a fiery sun! He held his head high in air, drew apart his monstrous jaws, while his teeth gleamed like ivory swords!

Then his words shot forth like the deep moan of the sea, or the wild breakers that dash against a rock-bound coast. Every tone fell like the command from a throne.

"I am monarch of the jungles! Who dares dispute my sway?

And he looked around haughtily.

"Man, in all his greatness, his genius, and his power, shrinks abashed in my presence!

"Amid the free hills, he cowers like a slave before me! My roar sounds to his coward soul like doom!

"Dare he meet me alone? Dare he crouch alone before my cave?

"Alas! I shame to tell it! I am no longer monarch! Oh, fell disgrace! Oh, woeful day! My scepter has departed!

"A Frenchman — what a wild race! — alone has dared to rule me! — to track me! — to kill me! One alone of the mighty millions that tread the earth — GIRARD — is now the true hero, and monarch of the jungles!

"His true nerve, fixed eye, and sure aim, make him the lion king!

"All hail to the only man who dared, alone, to track and kill me! — who dared to beard the lion even in his very den!"

The animals, in solemn acclaim, cried, "All

hail!" Even they, though against themselves, admired indomitable courage!

"How do the rest kill me? Bah! They dig deep holes; cover them with brush, sods, and earth, and take me in a miserable trap, in a sneaking manner.

"Or a hundred against one, they surround me with spears, and kill me! Is this fair?"

"No! no!" they all cried.

"But I repay them. At night, I devour their flocks! I keep them in perpetual fear!"

"Serves them right!" they all cried.

Then　　THE FROG

arose, and gave his experience.

"We are common game for all youngsters! No sooner do we pop up our heads, than out goes a stick, or stone, or shot! We are tormented by these human imps called children! And we have all found by bitter experience that man is cruel, relentless, thoughtless, and selfish!

serpents, and, on the sly, attacking man; but, like warrior chieftains, fiercely and openly striking its rattle-drums,—erect, king-like, undaunted!

The polite FROG for a moment shuddered at the fearful rattle; but recognizing his lordly person, begged the royal snake to proceed.

The RATTLESNAKE thus began:—

"Friends: we disdain, on the sly, like other snakes, to creep and crawl as if afraid of man!"

At these remarks, so derogatory to the other tribes of serpents, they raised their crested heads, and began to hiss furiously, whereupon the parliamentary FROG, astonished at this check on free speech, stamped his claw for silence, and looked around indignantly, like another Demosthenes.

"Friends," again resumed the stately Rattlesnake, "why does man fear me so? I am an open foe! My name strikes abject terror into every human heart; but I do not pounce upon them like the crafty tiger or the watchful lion. No! Before all the world I stand, and shake my war clarions. They have had the warning! Never again let man call our tribes sneaking, crawling, cowardly, treacherous! We advance to battle as boldly as did the old sea-kings of the north, as ready to take as to give, high-mettled and free.

"Coward man at our name slinks away in fear, and he is the snake! Instead of giving us open battle, he crawls and crouches in hiding, and pounces upon us suddenly, more like a sinuous reptile than a bold, fearless, upright man! We offer an open challenge for man either to accept or to retire. He offers a sly combat, trembling and shrinking with fear! Friends, we are a noble foe, always to the front, always ready for the fray. We sound our own battle-drums, as our battalions march to the fight; and we never yield till conquered,

while man often slinks away when the battle
is half fought, paralyzed with fear. And how
does he fight? Why, with dirty sticks and
stones, hurled at a distance, as if afraid of his
precious body, giving wounds, but too fearful
of receiving them.

"Look at his great height and bulk! Who
would believe he would fear such slight, delicate figures as we are? That we, scarcely a
twentieth of his size, would make him run!
Ay, run as if the devil was after him! and
make him sink on the ground fainting, like
an infant! A few rattles shakes his coward
heart; and all his pride, his dignity, his strength,
is cowed by a little serpent! What think you,
my friends, is man so godlike, after all? To
skulk from us in alarm and fear! No, indeed! Strike, my brethren, your warlike rattles, and let this puny man hear his coward
heart knock against his shaking sides at their
warlike notes! No drum is equal to its battle

sound! Who would think man was so long-legged, and made such strides?"

The animals all laughed heartily at this picture, and a great "Ha! ha! ha!" went forth at man's dread and weakness! They laughed till their sides ached, till exhausted, and old night shook in unison with them.

THE EAGLE.

Suddenly all the animals heard a rustling through the air. On looking up, they beheld a magnificent, immense-sized eagle, on his pinions, bearing down upon them. As he sailed majestically along, as though the very monarch of the air, you could see in his lordly bearing, his fearless mien, and his searching, powerful gaze, that he was the royal bird of Jove, free as the buoyant air, owning no mastery but God himself.

"Well, my friend," said the polite Frog, "tell us your sorrows."

"Friends: it is not often man has a chance

either to catch or shoot us, as our eyric is
amid the towering hills, or the lofty-pinnacled
cliffs. Where liberty breathes, amid the almost inaccessible rocks, is our free mountain
home. Our sweep is above his puny efforts,
and we disdain in our sublime flights to notice
him or his skill; yet still man, with his cunning, sometimes entraps us; and in his petty
wire cages clips our free wings' flight. There,
on little wooden perches, we sit down demure
and solemn in our narrow home, a melancholy
object of wonder. It is only in the boundless
air that we appear in our royal livery. Then,
with wide-spreading pinions, we are a glory
and a delight; and like a star of heaven we
stud the blue firmament like a winged god.
Freedom's self rushes with our wide-extended
wings, and gazes out of our bold piercing eyes.
Then our shrieks resound on the blasts, and
we pierce high heaven in our vast, extended,
upward flights. Behold our thunderbolt swoops

as we dive to earth like an avalanche of doom, and spitting our prey as if with an arrow of light!"

He had scarcely spoken, when up again he spread his airy flight, gave his clarion, warlike, piercing shriek, and they beheld him soaring like a wide-spreading sail, gloriously beautiful and poetically sublime.

THE ELEPHANT.

Hark to that lumbering tread! while the shrill, trumpet-like notes from his huge proboscis pierced the still, solemn air, like a battle-fife, giving notice of his approach. He advanced with slow yet majestic pace, shaking the solid earth by his heavy tread; and before their wondering eyes stood the mighty elephant, the modern mastodon, his sides gored with many a wound, his ivory tusk broken off, and every appearance of a great struggle in his manner, walk, and general bearing. He could scarcely breathe; but, with heroic effort, he dragged his heavy body along, and stood panting before the assembled tribes. He thus began:—

"Friends, of the great animal and insect race! I have had a very narrow escape for my life! I am just out of the toils; all the rest of my brethren are captives, base slaves to lordly man! But, thank God, I still am free!"

To this all the assembled tribes shouted an "All hail!"

"Only by herculean efforts did I break through all checks, and gain my freedom. Life is getting to be almost unbearable; for the way we are hunted and trapped for a little ivory leaves us but little peace in our native domains. Soon, very soon, we will become extinct, like our brother mastodon of old, whose mighty remains now only exist. Our great size, our immense strength, and our well-known sagacity and wide-awake intelligence, are nought against the superior cunning and art of man. His godlike intellect subdues our terrible ferocity and mighty power, till we become as docile and as harmless as little children, and are but straws in his hands; for he makes us beasts of burden, keeps us to hunt tigers for him, uses us as decoys to tame our wilder brothers, makes us add to his pomp and royal processions, conveys us around different countries to be a show and wonder to gaping crowds, learns us curious tricks for his money profit, and even in war hurls us against the enemy, while we are a very conspicuous mark for a thousand spears. With all our strength we are as little children in his hands, for he orders and we must obey! That little head of his, filled with the skill, knowledge, science, and art of a little god upon earth, conquers all; and we, who could sweep him out of existence with a slight blow of our ivory tusk, must submit to his puny body, be slaves to his lordly will, and remain a quiet captive forever.

"Friends, let me tell my story to your sympathetic ears, and then you will not envy my superior size, intelligence, and strength. We are as easily taken captive as the poor little mouse in the trap, or the foolish flies in the wire cages now invented to destroy them. Man now laughs at our immensity! He knows well enough his craft can offset it, and make him superior! What a satire, friends, is mere brute strength, without the keen, active, alert, thinking brain, to direct it! I own it, I feel cowed before man's superior intelligence; and our huge bulk is no more than a mere kitten to his superior skill! They make an inclosure of huge upright logs, strong enough and close enough to resist our mad fury when caught, and leave only one opening to drive us in. Near this opening fallen trees are so placed as to quickly fill up the gap, thus hedging us all around. The natives gather in great numbers, and form a wide circuit, gradually drive us en masse into this inclosure. I entered it, but shied at the last moment to the opening again, and broke my tusk in the fall against a huge log in my path, while all the hunters, furious at my escape, rained a forest of spears against me. Fear lent me wings, and, spite of all, I escaped.

"My brothers are subdued by hunters on tame elephants, who ride them down, badger them, and tie their hind legs to the logs, and so handle and whip them till they are willing slaves to his power!"

All the animals were very sad to see the fallen plight of this mighty beast,—to see his body bleeding from so many wounds, to see the crowning glory of his grand old head — his ivory glory — broken; that tusk ennobled by many a victory over the savage, remorseless tiger,—that shield for defence,—forever destroyed. They all offered up a solemn prayer for his safe return to his native forests, and a speedy recovery from his many wounds.

THE BUFFALO.

Hark to that deep, grumbling, threatening roar! All the animal tribes suddenly started at the fearful sound,—when, with eyes all aflame, shaggy head tossed defiantly, upleaps into their very midst a gigantic bull buffalo, a gory stream raining down his sides, while a feathered arrow stood out from his shaggy hide. He was puffing and blowing with his frantic leapings to be in time.

"Well," said our polite FROG, "how does the king of the prairies wide? How does the wild glory of the desert plains?"

Another smothered roar, that sounded like distant rumbling thunder, while his eyes grew fiercer in their wrath, as he shook his huge bulk in proud disdain as he gave them a history of his wrongs.

"Look at me, almost pinned to earth by an Indian's barbed arrow!—my life-blood flowing through man's brutality! We expect the wild

Indian to use us to supply his wants, for we are his natural food upon the plains; but, far away, from the distant cities they come in throngs to hunt us, often in mere wantonness, or to boast of their wondrous shooting skill. Do they not have their towns, villages, and cities? Do they not have their oxen, pigs, and poultry? Can not they leave the lone prairies for us to roam in?—the wild home given us by the good God? No! Man is never satisfied till he destroys all he can lay his savage hands upon!

"Alas! after my free body is slain, he desecrates the carcass, strips off our shaggy hide to minister to his luxury and comfort; and our fell destroyers can keep it as a memento of our fallen pride, and a trophy of his victory! When we are dust, he can revel in warmth in our noble covering!

"In the rivalries of hunting parties, we are destroyed by thousands, or are driven headlong over rocky precipices in our terrible sudden flight, to perish mangled amid torture and groans,—often trampling each other to death in our sudden hurry to escape; and soon we will disappear like the great mastodon of old, whose remains man so often digs up in his scientific researches.

"We have no chance of escape, since the terrible, unerring, deadly, far-sighted, repeating rifle, strikes us from afar, to our ruin and death; and we, free, wild roamers of the desert, will fast disappear beneath their murderous shots! Awe and lamentation goes forth from all my tribes!

"Animals, is it not hard that soon their cities will cover those free, wild, desert plains, sacred to our glorious tread? That the noise of the hammer and forge will resound where our free bellowings shook the affrighted air, and reverberated through the hills and forests and along the plains? That where we were monarchs, their poor drudges of horses, asses, mules, and oxen will tread,—those slaves of man defiling the earth where we free dwellers once trod?

"Alas! soon only in tradition will our glorious herds live!—those herds that once assembled in droves of tens of thousands, shaking the lordly earth with our mighty tread!"

All the animals pitied his sad fate, and a wail went forth in the solemn chambers of the night air for the future fate of the pride and glory of the great American prairies.

Then

THE FROG

arose, and gave his experience.

"We are common game for all youngsters! No sooner do we pop up our heads, than out goes a stick, or stone, or shot! We are tormented by these human imps called children! And we have all found by bitter experience that man is cruel, relentless, thoughtless, and selfish!

"So let us band together, and devise ways and means to better protect ourselves."

So Mr. FLY took down the minutes of the meeting, and it was handed throughout the earth, that all the animal tribes might read it.

Then they all sat down to a great feast that had been prepared for them, after which they had many dancings, leapings, flyings, tumblings, singings, and whistlings.

After all their natural wants were satisfied, the poor old Cow begged the company to listen to a few of her remarks.

The polite FROG assented.

The Cow then said:—

"Noble fellow-creatures: A man bold, per-sistent, honest, and fearless, has arisen to avenge our wrongs, and to tame this needless brutality in man, to check his ruthless excesses, and restrain him to proper decency and mercy. As the champion of the animal race, he deserves our best wishes, our highest regard, our purest homage. And before this meeting breaks up, let us all arise and give one sublime, glorious 'All hail!' to BERGH."

They arose, in great solemnity, and awoke the slumbering echoes of the night with an "All hail! all hail!" till the woods around re-echoed "All hail! all hail!"

The MOCKING-BIRD, who was the poet of the animal tribes, begged their indulgence while he recited this piece of poetry, his own composition.

The polite FROG assented.

> Animals have a right to live,
> Eat, drink, and sleep, in peace.
> A title to such joys the Creator gives,
> Till death gives them release.
> We ask only mercy of man,—
> To treat us with humanity.
> Few pleasures are our span;
> Let us enjoy them without cruelty.

Just as day was beginning to dawn, the party broke up, and all was still again.

They then departed each to his home.

So you see, my children, animals, birds, insects, and fishes, have as many trials and sorrows as man.

THE

FEAST OF FLOWERS.

N old man sat by the Christmas fire, surrounded by his children and grand-children, and amused them by telling a story, called the FEAST OF FLOWERS.

You must imagine the FLOWERS to have tongues to talk with, and eyes to see, and minds to think and compare.

You must think they are human FLOWERS, for the time. This is not so, you know; but we put eyes and tongues into the FLOWERS, to make them amusing and instructive.

On a bright June day, there was to be a

Feast of Flowers, and a prize was to be given to the most beautiful.

So all the Flowers in the world were there, fresh with the morning dews, all blooming and expanded, gay and brilliant in the sunbeams.

They sat beneath a wide-spreading oak, near a lovely stream, so that they might take a cooling sip now and then, to refresh their beauty and revive their drooping spirits.

One of the Fairies was to be judge. They piled soft mosses together, and all the Flowers reclined upon them.

The majestic

PEONY

first arose, with an air of regal grandeur and an imposing bearing, large and full-blown,—a real giantess among the blossoms.

"Am I not gorgeous? Behold my size, my splendor, my ample rotundity!"

"Bah!" said little Mignonette, under her breath; "a great overgrown lubber!"

Next the

SUNFLOWER

arose, and thus addressed them:—

"Behold my lofty stem! Am I not regal, like a golden crown? See how I am always turned to the sun's eye, as I fondly show my face to him, his golden kisses floating like a wreath upon my forehead.

"Can you match me in state and dignity, as I o'ertop all the FLOWERS?"

"Yes! a big beanpole," said little JUMP-UP-JOHNNY.

"A good handle for a broomstick!" said little CREEPING-CHARLEY.

"Ah!" said little VIOLET, "I am out of place amongst so many grand nabobs! I wish I had stayed at home."

The little

JUMP-UP-JOHNNY

arose, and, with a merry twinkle of his eye, said:—

"Ah! can you match my vigor, parti-colored elegance, and late bloom? You see me peep forth even in the lap of winter, when the big PEONY consumptive is strewn upon the gale. When these big boasters have all decayed, I am seen on many a winter's morn as young as ever. You know rare gems are always small in size! If I am only a wee thing, I am full of hardy life.

"Come, good FAIRY, I want the prize!"

All the FLOWERS laughed at his pertness, and clapped their hands in sport. In great good humor he sat down, almost out of sight, amid those huge mosses.

Then a great

CACTUS

got up, clumsy and slow, with pompous dignity, and said,—

"Behold my beauty and glory!"

"Oh, yes! a glory of green prickles!" said Miss SWEET ALYSSIUM.

"All body and no head!" said little DAISY.

Mortified at these half-heard interruptions, he sat down, and wrapped himself in his dignity.

While they were thus discussing, a swarm of BEES kept buzzing around, and with great difficulty the FAIRY kept them off with her wand; but a saucy BEE dodged her staff, lit upon a plump ROSE, and stung her to the quick.

She screamed, in her agony,—

"Oh, you ugly BEE!"

All the FLOWERS gathered around her, and, with gentle pity, soothed her wounded feelings.

The air was so sweet with so many perfumes, that swarms of FLIES and INSECTS kept floating around, all eager to get a sip.

Once they all rushed in pell-mell; but the FAIRY, with her wand, made a terrible breeze, and drove them off.

The big PEONY could not stand the shock,

and its petals were strewn upon the wind, and all the Flies had a feast that day.

After this disturbance was all over, a pale, stately

LILY

uprose, dainty white, and exquisitely perfumed, —a very dandy flower,—so tall and elegant, so nice and neat, the *bon-ton* in grace, refinement, and delicacy. She was the very *elite* of flowers, and the pride of the aristocracy.

She said little, but looked around as if her presence alone was worth the prize. A hum of admiration greeted her. Pleased at this quiet homage, she gracefully sat down again.

A gaudy

TULIP

arose, and was just about to speak, when a tiny Serpent crawled out of its petals. What a scampering there was of Flowers!

The Fairy hit him with her wand, and killed him.

"Oh!" said D<small>AISY</small>, "what a precious *love* you keep within your bosom! What a *beauty* for a companion!"

And they all laughed.

Miss T<small>ULIP</small> pouted in disdain; and, confused, sat down.

Then little

BUTTERCUP

jumped up, and said:—

"Give me the prize! Am I not a golden crown? Are not crowns right royal? Then make me queen!"

"And make me king!" said little

DANDELION.

"Am I not a *dandy lion?*—and therefore ought to be *king* (not of beasts, but) of *flowers*."

All were merry with these conceits.

The wax-like

CAMELIA

next appeared,—a drawing-room exquisite,— and, with languid speech, said:—

"What need of boasting? You can see for yourself my charms! How I am prized, and sought for in the realms of fashion!"

"Fashion be hanged!" said plain APPLE-BLOSSOM.

"For not patronizing you, I suppose, Miss SAUCEBOX!" retorted Miss CAMELIA.

Then the

ORANGE-BLOSSOM

spoke in her own behalf:—

"Young, coy maidens, choose me on the bridal-day. I deck the head of Beauty; and the vestal bride hails me as her sweetest ornament. I ever attend the most holy rite of marriage; and my unusual claims must be allowed!"

"Yes!" said an old lonely flower (BACHELORS' BUTTON), "we allow you look as if you had the jaundice!" (referring to oranges.)

And he laughed at his own wit.

A THISTLE

then arose, and said:—

"I claim the prize! A great warlike nation has chosen me as its emblem,—old Scotia, of ancient renown."

"Is that so?" said

FLEUR-DE-LIS.

"I dispute the claim. Old Gaul, all fight, makes me her emblem-flower!"

And the LILY of France proudly looked around.

"Ah!" said old

STINKWEED,

"don't put on such airs!"

And she turned up her nose, in high disdain,—while all the FLOWERS looked askance at her, and wondered at her impudence.

"Ah!" said little

FORGET-ME-NOT,

"I am wrongly named; for you see all forget me! I am completely overlooked!"

"Well," said a gay

HONEYSUCKLE,

"I see you don't forget yourself!"

And they all smiled.

"What time is it?" they all cried. "Who has a timepiece?"

"Why, I have, and 'tis only

FOUR O'CLOCK,"

said that sweet and very beautiful flower; and she laughed at her own pun.

"Look!

DAN CUPID

is around; and he has just hit one of the flowers with an arrow; and there

LOVE-LIES-BLEEDING.

"Ah, what would the ladies do without me? Who so well supplies their dainty little feet?" said Miss

LADY-SLIPPER.

"I know I am the ladies' pet, but not the Flowers'," said old

MULLEIN-STALK;

"so please step down, and get out, and make room for old

DUTCHMAN'S PIPE,

who is just arising."

He looked around, with comical gravity, and asked who wanted to smoke.

"I'll give you a leaf!" said

TOBACCO-BLOSSOM.

"Come, choose me!" said

BLUE-BELLS,

"and I will set all the air a-ringing merry peals!"

"Don't you want silver fringes to your robes?" asked the

VIRGINIA WHITE-FRINGE.

"If you do, I can supply you all; so let me be queen!"

"Ah! you want my blossoms to light your fire!" said

BURNING-BUSH.

"Yes; fringes are very good, but you want tassels with them. I am in that line of business, and can supply them at first cost, for I manufacture my own goods," said Miss

TASSEL-FLOWER.

"Would you like to keep a hive of Bees, and sip most delicious honey? If you do, make me queen!" said Miss

HONEYSUCKLE,

"and I'll supply all with most exquisite perfumes."

"I dare not offer myself," said the

SENSITIVE PLANT,

"for I always have the chills and fever, and never get clear of the shakes."

"My friends, are you in love, or in sorrow? Let me console you!" said little

HEART'S-EASE.

"I will be your family physician!"

"Do you want a plume to adorn a prince? I am at your service!" said Miss

PRINCESS-FEATHER.

"Do you wish a stiff breeze, to brush away the mosquitoes? Choose me, then!" said the

WIND-FLOWER.

"Do you wish a fancy kite, to amuse the dull hours with? I'll supply most curious specimens!" said the

KITE-FLOWER.

"Come, let me be king! I'll supply beautiful granite to build your palaces!" said the

ROCK-PLANT.

"Ladies, do you not want a genuine dandy? — a natural exquisite,— to dance with, to adorn your parlors, and have a nice tete-a-tete with?" said the

COCKSCOMB.

"Ah, sweet belles of society! Let me supply you with shining mirrors, to reflect your gorgeous beauty!" said Miss

VENUS' LOOKING-GLASS.

"Do choose me, and I'll ever be at your beck and nod!"

And she smiled in fawning flattery upon them.

"Do you dwell in the wild forests, amid savage Indian tribes? Then choose me! I'll bring down your boldest enemy with my aim and shot!" said the true marksman,

SCARLET INDIAN-SHOT.

"Dear little ladies, you know the sweet song, 'Up in a Balloon'? Well, if you wish me as your queen, you can sail every day amid the stars, and truly make that song real!" said Miss

BALLOON-VINE.

"You all need vials, to keep your precious perfumes from spoiling! At my factory I have some beautiful specimens of rare workmanship, —very stylish ornaments for the boudoir. Ladies, you must make me your king!" said great

BLUE-BOTTLE.

"Ye flowers from Turkey, do you wish a ruler?—a right royal lord?—one born to the purple?—one of the truest blue blood? I can accommodate you!" said the haughty

SWEET SULTAN-FLOWER.

"Ladies and gentlemen: I have just imported a great variety of new and attractive patterns of wall-paper. Please examine my stock before purchasing elsewhere. Your rooms will look lively and pleasant!" said the

WALL-FLOWER.

"Do you wish to enjoy all the delights of the fresh morning?—the sunny air?—the brightness and the glow of early day? Then I am your queen!" said

MORNING-GLORY.

"Don't you want a staff?—oh, ye fighting Flowers!—a real shillalah? Are ye lame, and need a crutch, oh, ye rheumatic Flowers? Do ye need a policeman's club, to crack skulls with?—so fashionable in our great cities! Here I am, ready for a brawl!" said bold, daring

HERCULES'-CLUB.

And, with a terrific whack, he came down upon the trembling earth, while all the Flowers looked up in fear.

"Do you want some melons to feed your pet serpents with?—especially you, Miss TULIP! Here I have a supply, so delicious and juicy 'twill make your mouths water!—the genuine Mountain Sweet, and the old-fashioned heavily netted Nutmeg!"

And a hiss issued from the opened fangs of the

SNAKE-MELON.

"Ah, ye old maids of Flowers! Are ye tired of single blessedness? Would ye no longer be called spinsters? Let me console you!" said little

SWEET-WILLIAM,

with a twinkle in his merry eye.

"Would you make a noise in the world, like our long-winded orators? Do you want a plentiful supply of blarney,—especially ye, oh politicians! I am full of gas! Would you make your parlors brilliant with gorgeous lights?—make your stores and streets shine like the day? I have a factory at home, and an abundant supply on hand!" said the

GAS-PLANT.

"Are ye sad and mournful? Come, walk beneath my melancholy shades, and muse on the nothingness of life, the certainty of death, and the vanity of all things! Plant me amid your tombs, and let me adorn your cemeteries!" said the

CYPRESS-VINE.

"Oh, I am to be your king! I belong to the most holy Church, and can supply you with a real prince cardinal!—first-class, ready-made, of the purest lineage!" said the high-born

CARDINAL-FLOWER.

"Are you going to a party?—a grand reception?—or to be a bride? Do you want rich robes to array in,—oh, ye vain, dressy, showy Flowers? I am a real

SATIN-FLOWER,

and will furnish you twenty yards of the best foreign importation at the shortest notice, warranted not to fade!"

"Do you want a glass of cooling drink, in the heats of summer?—some ice to make ice-cream? Or who is so useful as me, to soothe your heated brains,—your perspiring bodies,—in the dry and arid month of August?" said little

ICE-PLANT.

"Who bathes the Flowers in the arid heats of summer? In the terrible droughts, I will drop into your nostrils, and bathe your brows, like manna from the clouds. I must be your queen, or else I'll let you all dry and wither up!" said little

DEW-PLANT.

"Oh, ye sighing lovers! Do you want a quiet nook to bill and coo in?—a retired shade where you can pour out all the melodies of the heart, undisturbed by the rude world, and nestle together heart to heart, like cooing doves? I will be your

LOVE-GROVE,

to please your amorous desires."

"Do you want to get into a tantrum, go on a spree, have a real jamboree, and make things lively all around you? Then I am your man!" said the

PASSION-FLOWER.

"Is it cloudy? Is it rainy? Does the sun hide himself, as in the night? Do you always want to be in the light? Is it misty, dull, and gloomy? Would you have all things look

cheerful, sunny, and gay? Then I am old
Sol's rival; and the

SUN-PLANT

will supply his place."

"Do you want a ladder to climb to the luscious fruit?—to get to the leafy shades of the
forest-trees,—oh, ye Flowers of the earth?
Jacob can, I think, lend you his ladder!"
said Mr.

JACOB'S LADDER.

"Do you wish to be immortal?—never to
perish? Then get beneath my wing!" said
the

EVERLASTING-FLOWER.

"I will make your life perpetual!"

"Do you like creams and custards?—nice
omelettes? I can furnish eggs of all sizes and
colors!" said Miss

EGG-PLANT.

And the eyes of all the Flowers sparkled
in anticipation of a feast.

"Do you lack wisdom? Do you love learning? Would you understand philosophy? Then let me be your king!" said the

SAGE-PLANT.

And he looked upon the Flowers with majestic dignity and solemn presence, as if all creation was his royal self.

"Do you always want to live in clover?—always with the dance, and song, and feast? Then I am the most delightful, most fragrant

SWEET-SCENTED CLOVER,

to perfume you all, and make you as happy as kings!"

"Oh, ye bachelors!—ye forlorn and disconsolate lonely ones! Ye who have to sew on your own buttons!—do your own mending and darning!—with no sweet faces to smile around you!—no little darlings to love you!—your hearts withered for lack of the sweet influences of marriage! Have you lost a button,

and would find another? Come here, and take
me!" said old

BACHELORS' BUTTON.

"I'll sew them all on at the shortest notice, as
I am a born tailor."

"Do you want consolation?—or are you in
the dumps? Have you got the blues? Are
you dying with ennui? Does the world go
wrong with you? Have you a note unpaid?
Are you dunned by a creditor? Does your
boot pinch your toes? Or is your coffee cold
at the breakfast? Or has your wife given
you a curtain lecture? Here am I, the

BALM-OF-GILEAD,

a soother of all your sorrows."

"Do you want a guardian?—a night watch-
man?—a keeper? Here I am!" said brave,
sturdy, warlike

HEDGE-HOG,

looking around, like an old warrior armed to
the teeth.

"Yes, and are you dry?—are you athirst? Let me supply you with the

HORN OF PLENTY.

"Ah! would you play the hypocrite, and seem soft-hearted? Would you impose on the sympathy of others? Are you at a funeral, and you look cold and hard-hearted to all, and seem without compassion? A little of my

JOB'S TEARS

will make you more human."

"Has Joseph, or any other poor fellow, lost his coat? Come to my tailor-shop, and get a new one, at little cost. I sell everything on a hard money basis!" said

JOSEPH'S COAT.

"Do you want to deceive the world, and hide your love? Let me surround you with my mist, and obscure you!" said Miss

LOVE-IN-A-MIST.

"Do you want to tantalize your lover?—to have a real lover's quarrel,—that you may have the exquisite satisfaction of making it up again? I will lend you, for the occasion, a little of my real genuine

LOVE-IN-A-PUFF."

"Oh, ye churchmen! Are times hard? Is money scarce, and business dull? Come, bring me your monks (not monkies!), and, free of charge, I'll give them all a pretty hood!" said

MONKSHOOD,

"as I am of a religious turn of mind, and a devotee."

"Oh, ye refined lady Flowers! Do you want a popular scent, at little cost? I can supply you plenty!" said

MUSK-PLANT.

"Are you solemn, sedate, sad, and musing, and wish a plain sympathetic companion for a wife?—one not fond of pleasure and fashion, domestic in her taste, who always prefers home to the pleasures of the world?—a helpmeet,

not a spendmeet! One who is willing to adapt
her expenses to your station and your fortunes?
—one of the true breed of real women, who
prefers duty to show, and virtue to applause?
Then choose my

MOURNING BRIDE."

"You have no poet to sing your charms,
oh, ye Flowers! Do you want an aristocratic
Court poet-laureate, like Tennyson? Or a sim-
ple, sweet songster, like Burns? A picturesque
and romantic poet, like Scott? Or a passion-
ate and ideal rhymer, like Byron? A contem-
plative, studious, natural poet, like Bryant?
Or a weird, spiritual one, like Shelley or Poe?
Do you wish one—all—for love and the heart,
like Moore?—skilled in all the graces of society, and exquisite in warm and ardent melodies? Perhaps you prefer plain, downright,
earnest, manly Whittier? Or the deep, clarion-
like tones of Campbell? Or the dreamy lux-
uries of Coleridge? Or the soul-like strains of

Hood? Or the rough, every-day songs, of Whitman? Or would ye dream of a heaven and a hell with Dante? Or laugh and grow fat with Hudibras? I possess the divine afflatus, —to the manor born, as the saying is!" spoke up little poetic

DAISY,

his sweet face shining like a morning star.

"Have you lost a nose in a quarrel, or by a cancer? Or got it knocked off by a policeman's club, oh, ye drinking, fighting Flowers? I keep an assortment always on hand, ready-made,— the bold, hooked Roman; the curved, patriotic aquiline; the feminine retroussee; the turned-up celestial; the pug, and the snub; the rum-bottle kind; the broad, secretive nose; and the long, suspicious variety; as well as the perfect, re- fined, straight, chiselled Grecian. I can supply Turk, Christian, or Jew, as I keep an extensive assortment always on hand!" said

PROBOSCIS FLOWER.

"Do you want to please the variety of your lady-love? I'll lend you a little trembling, a slight quiver!" said little

QUAKING-GRASS.

"Do you ever brush your rooms, to keep them neat, and clean, and tidy? Or are you all slatterns?" asked the

SCOTCH BROOM.

"If you are over nice, old Scotia is the place to buy them."

"Have you a spite against your sister Flowers? Put me into their sleeping ears!" said the venomous

SPIDER-FLOWER,

and I will frighten them almost to death."

"Do you want some fireworks on the fourth of July?—something brilliant! Here am I, always ready to go up!" said

SWEET ROCKET.

"Ah! are you misanthropic, cold, and un-social, and would not be bothered? Carry me

in your button-hole, and I'll warrant you oblivion from all acquaintances. I'll keep both
sheriff and policeman from you, from all duns
and beggings, reporters and canvassers!" said

TOUCH-ME-NOT.

"Oh, ye pale, cadaverous-looking Flowers!—
thin and consumptive! Oh, ye worn-out society
belles, *passe* to the world! A little rouge
would make you pretty and attractive; and 'tis
fashionable, as you all know!" said

VENUS' PAINT-BRUSH.

"Ah, sweet maidens! Ye fair vestals!
Would ye recline in Nature's arbor?—a natural
alcove,—alone with your coy modesty and
shy purity? Come, and enter my

VIRGIN'S BOWER."

"Would you be old or young? Choose!
For I can make you either, or both!" said

YOUTH AND OLD AGE.

"Look!" said the ROSE; "here is little VIO-
LET! See how quiet she is! How modest

and retiring! Always acting with propriety, and so well behaved! Make her queen!"

"Oh, yes!" said Miss POPPY. "Too quiet to rule such unruly subjects! Let her be the queen's lapdog!—her pet!—and recline at her feet!"

"You are too presumptuous!" said the ROSE.

"Am I?" retorted Miss POPPY. "Beware! or I'll squirt my juice into your eye, and put you asleep!"

"Bah!" said the ROSE. "Keep your poison for the Chinese!"

Just then a big SUNFLOWER fell off its stem, and crushed the ROSE's toe. Crazy with the pain, she begged Miss POPPY to put her to sleep.

She looked so sweet and blushing in her slumber, her soft breath was so deliciously perfumed, she looked so plump and rounded, so exquisitely colored, that all the Flowers crowded around her, and gazed at her in deep admiration; and all, with one accord, hailed her QUEEN!

In their excitement, they jostled one another, and fell upon the ROSE's thorns. Their screaming awoke her; and seeing so many bleeding bodies and so many torn robes, she was frightened; but so sweetly begged their forgiveness, that all were charmed, and again hailed her QUEEN!

So, from that day to this, the ROSE is QUEEN OF FLOWERS!

"The prize! the prize!" all cried, at once.

The Fairy took from beneath her robe a tiny crystal vase, beautifully embroidered all over with gold, and, with a charming smile, offered it to the blushing ROSE, who, with a noble courtesy, accepted it.

The Fairy said:—

"When thou appearest in Beauty's boudoir, be thou always placed in this lovely vase, that thou may'st be seen in noblest state, befitting the QUEEN OF FLOWERS.

All arose, and cheers of welcome echoed all around.

The Fairy then spread before the Flowers the most delicious dews, the most sparkling rains, the fairest sunbeams, the most protecting cloud-lings, the sweetest perfumes, the most gorgeous colors, the most exquisite shapes; and told them to sip to their hearts' content.

She gave them, also, the richest moulds to robe their bodies in.

Thus ends the FEAST OF FLOWERS.

So you see they all chattered, each in her turn. Each had a virtue of her own,—some peculiar gift,—and each had power to help the others.

So you see, even amid Flowers there was a world of their own, apart from all the world,— a succession of enjoyments, uses, and gifts,— making them supreme in their sphere.

Each Flower acted and talked its best, so as to gain the prize; but the ROSE was as modest, as beautiful, as charming, with that air of well-bred ease betokening true gentility; with health, and strength, and purity, to give high command, and that right royal condescension to make it loved and popular, and all the Flowers' hearts went out to her insensibly, before they were aware of it.

The ROSE was the VENUS among the Flowers, —born for sweet sympathy, born for divine fondling, amorous embraces, and everlasting love.

THE

FOUR ANGELS.

A DREAM.

YOUNG GIRL told this dream to her mother, just as it appeared to her.

I thought I was reclining amid a bed of flowers, on the bank of a large stream.

The moon was just overhead, and gleaming in dancing brightness on the wavy waters.

Not a being or animal, bird or insect, was to be seen. All was a holy quiet, a serene repose.

I was reclining, full length, with my eyes upturned to the heavens.

I thought overhead hung four clouds,—two

of silver and two of gold,—spread upon the sky like balls of fire.

They seemed to open, and four beautiful angels, with their wings outspread, fluttered on the edge of these beautiful clouds.

They shook their wings at me and smiled. One had lovely silver wings, another crimson, a third gold, and the fourth seemed of a violet shade.

They commenced to fly round and round these clouds, then half dived toward the earth; again, in single line, flitted through the air; then they seemed to form wing and wing together, wheeling in circles round and round each other; again, for a while, they seemed to float motionless on their outstretched wings. At last they came floating directly overhead, and hung upon the air in a charmed circle, and, one after another, thus whispered softly in my ear.

THE FIRST ANGEL.

I am the Spirit of Hope. Into your being

let me breathe my visions, to make your life beautiful in the golden joys of the future.

In the darkest hour you'll see me perched above your soul, to lift you beyond life's cares, —make you forget its sorrows in the bright halos of a hope beyond the grave.

I am God's silver lining to the black clouds of life.

In every darkness you'll see me radiating through the void; breathing light and joy through the blackness,—making every care pass away.

My spirit ever wanders o'er the dreariest hours, and, with sweet illuminations, I dispel them, and hurl into oblivion all the gloomy past.

Look! on thy head I place one of my silver crowns, to ever remind thee of me.

Remember, in thy hour of gloom, to place it on thy brow. It is a charm potent to banish all grief away.

She then uprose, and, floating upon the air, ascended to the silver cloud, and disappeared within its airy fleece.

A SECOND ANGEL

then whispered, I am the

SPIRIT OF FAITH.

In the dark uncertainties of life, I breathe truth and constancy within the soul. In the troubled breast I instil confidence. In the sad, forlorn spirit, I speak of a brighter joy, a holier life beyond the grave.

My presence ever gives FAITH in man, in God, in hereafter, in heaven. Without me, life becomes a cold skeptic, a forlorn hope, a faithless and heartless realm of uncertainties, a realm of doubts and fears.

With me fly half of life's doubts. With me comes a radiant belief, a hopeful joy, a bright anticipation, a glorious promise of a heaven hereafter.

With my twin sister HOPE, who has just

flown to her silver home, we make the life of man blessed by our radiant sunshine, dispelling all doubts, uncertainties, skepticisms, and unbeliefs.

We are God's prime ministers in the heavens, directing the soul of man upward to Him.

In the dark night we are life's moonbeams. In disease, poverty, and sorrow, we are guardian helpmates.

We make men have faith in each other, wives in their husbands, parents in their children, partners in their business, the husbandmen in their harvests, and all in their ventures.

I make men certain that there is virtue, goodness and truth, trust and confidence, chastity and honor, fidelity and constancy.

We are the finger-posts of time, to show the way to heaven. We are all light, and on our brows we wear the Diadem of Immortality.

We are the custodians of the crowns of heaven.

Sweet child! We each bind on your brows a diadem.

And she placed a second crown upon my head. Then she also ascended, and was lost in the second silver cloud.

A THIRD ANGEL

whispered, I am the

SPIRIT OF MERCY.

I melt the hardened heart. I soothe the criminal. I soften the callous soul. I gently instil my love, my pity, in the soul of man, to make him forgiving, kind, and forbearing.

Life, without me, would be a breathing horror; with me, it becomes a dove-like peace, a calm wave, a cloudless sky, a serene hope, a fervent faith.

We see a bow of promise in the air,—a radiant belief of forgiveness hereafter. I lift from life its load of agony, and angels beckon up to heaven.

Mercy! 'tis the star of Hope that shines afar,

amid disease, plagues, ruin, and chaos; amid murder, lust, rapine, blood, and slaughter.

It rises o'er the ruins of life, the pitying eye of GOD, directing us within its beams to a temple in the heavens everlasting, where each and all can find rest and shelter,—where each and all will be blessed in the Divine forgiveness.

I instil within the soul of man a spirit of gentleness and of peace. I unbend the bent bow of vengeance, with its fierce shaft of death, and even on the gibbet I oft pardon the criminal.

In war, I spare the victim at my foot, and receive nations again in the bonds of amity. I soothe with pardon some lost stricken child of sin; and to millions who are ready to strike, I say, let him who is guiltless cast the first stone!

O'er the heavens I ever bend the rainbow of promise and of peace. I ever radiate Hope and sunshine, and bless many a wounded heart, and open the way to heaven for many a lost stray sinner from the fold of Christ.

Then she placed a GOLDEN CROWN upon my head, and ascended to the golden cloud that lay on the sky.

THE FOURTH ANGEL

whispered, I am the

SPIRIT OF CHARITY.

I possess a soul of pity, boundless as are the wants of man. I open man's heart to overflow with gifts to the needy and the poor.

Where'er I go, tears of thanks flow in homage to my generous soul.

In the hour of want I move like a pitying God, to shelter the outcast, to clothe the naked, to feed the hungry; and make the lone and sad heart, wasted body, and despairing soul, all a joy in their satisfied needs, their general comforts, and heartfelt sympathies.

I breathe only to be kind and generous, to

make all happy, all satisfied, all content. Where I go, blessings, thanks, and prayers, surround me.

All kneel to me as the only GOD on earth, that can stay the hand of want and despair.

I feed the body, and so soothe the soul, gladden the heart, and make the mind at ease.

I stay back the gaunt hand of famine, and rouse the world to give of their over-fullness to our starving brother.

I dwell not in the halls of revelry and of wealth. No! you see me amid disease and filth, amid rags and poverty, in the low humble hut, in the lonely street, on the broad plains, where want and care dwell; where gaunt famine strides with skeleton form, hollow visage, palsied gait, and coughing utterance.

There, where sorrow, and misery, and despair, attend as weird spirits, to destroy and punish; there, like a light from heaven, I radiate my presence, and make that scene of horror glow with the Sun of Hope.

I weep for the sin and folly of man. I melt with pity for the poor deserted children of God. I am radiant with bliss, when I can aid and soothe their wants.

Sweet young child! Let me place a fourth crown upon thy head. Ever, when thou gazest upon dire poverty, wear this crown, and thy heart will melt with pity for their woes; thou wilt then open thy purse to their needs, and so receive the smiles of heaven.

I am the last spirit that will whisper to thee; yet remember, without my crown thou art lost, not only on this earth, but also in heaven.

Sweet charity will cancel many a deed of sin, and God will recompense thee hereafter, for the open hand, the open heart, and the open soul.

Wear, sweet child of clay, these four diadems of Immortality. Let them link together as one, and thy life will pass nobly on earth, nobly at death, and still more nobly shine on high.

When thou goest forth in the world, let these crowns be as the Charms of Heaven. Let them glitter on thy pathway, and radiate their pure chastened light on the wretched, poor, despised, and forgotten children of men.

Then you can be an Angel even as we are, with shining wings, and a free unrestrained flight in all the ages through the vast illimitable reaches of God's domain.

The Angel floated above me, and entered the second golden cloud. Then all grew dark again!

THE

HAUNTED CASTLE.

Y children asked me to tell them a story of a Haunted Castle.

On a gentle slope of a hill, embowered in stately forest trees, uprose a grey castle, made of granite, turretted with towers, moss-grown, and green with ivy.

It looked as if it had stood there a thousand years,—a quaint old castle, hoary with time, strange, solemn, and lonely.

As you approached it, all was still as death; not a sound was heard,—no sign of life was seen around it.

It seemed to be deserted by man and beast; almost forgotten by Time itself. Yet strange scenes were there enacted, strange orgies had passed within its halls, wild music had waked the echoes of the night around its walls, and dancing feet had made old Time enamored with their lightness and gay abandon.

The feast and dance had raged within, with beauty, wealth, and youth,—with brilliancy of dancing lights, the sparkle of many a wine, and the glories of all the earth were once heaped within its vast domain; yet, now, it stood as if a sentinel to mark the ages as they passed away, shunned by all, a fear to the peasantry around it, apparently accursed by God and man.

A single road led to it from the surrounding country.

On a still, quiet eve, I urged my horse, as if by instinct, through this bewildering maze of woods, till, in the soft twilight, this castle loomed

up like a strange dream,—a weird, almost spectral, mass of turrets.

I dismounted, tied my horse to a tree, and
roamed a while around its vast proportions.

Here, thought I, was the home of the demi-
gods of earth, the lords of this lower world,—
some great race renowned in the annals of time;
yet, from those stony piles no voice said yes to
my musings.

Still there was a look around it, as if some
skill and art kept this old castle strong and fine
with time; some legacy, thought I, kept it in
repair, or it was a solemn heirloom to some de-
pendant family to see to its care in the ages,
as long as one was left to minister to its proper
repair; and I was right.

I ascended on foot to the great door of the
castle, and rang the bell, which sounded solemnly, strangely, weirdly, amid those dense forests.

Each tree seemed, to my musing fancy, as
the haunt of a demon; and I thought queer

voices mingled with the dying cadences of that solitary, lonely bell.

Slowly the door opened, and a face almost as old as the trees around, a pale cadaverous face, wrinkled with the cares of time, with hair like the driven snow, peeped forth in a cranny of the door.

"What is wanted of the haunted castle? What intruder dares to disturb the sacred silence of this old home of a race long passed away? Who art thou?"

And a keen, dark, penetrating glance, conned me o'er and o'er. At her feet, I saw a savage hound lay crouched, his glancing eyes fierce as the tiger of the jungles.

I told her chance had led me here, and curiosity and wonder had held me spell-bound. I was a stranger from foreign lands; and at the inn far below, I had heard strange, queer tales, of the haunted castle.

I longed to pierce its secret, and behold its inner walls. A faint smile lit up the old face.

"You are not, then, a native of this country?"

"No; from far America!"

The old crone mused a moment, and then the door swung open wide, and I passed within,— the hound eyeing me almost with a human glance, so keen and penetrating was his look. 'Twas satisfactory, however, for he sat quietly down again near me.

I opened my purse to the old woman, and asked her for its history.

She eyed me keenly again.

"Wilt thou swear not to repeat it till thou art again in thy own home, across the sea?— never to whisper to any one around these domains what I tell thee?"

"I swear!"

She solemnly answered "Amen" to this; and bade me sit in a large old chair, made in generations gone by. A dim light, almost spectral, flashed in misty radiance around an inner hall, wainscotted in oak, filled with pictures of knights in armor, and ladies in court costumes of times long gone by.

A huge carved chair stood alone.

"Look!" said she. "'Tis the Chair of Blood! Accursed! accursed!"

And she rocked herself to and fro, as if old memories of the past had stirred her soul.

"I am the last,—the last of the descendants of a once haughty line.

My fathers and forefathers have for ages watched this castle. With my death it passes to stranger hands, and servile help will soon let all go to neglect and ruin.

This thought makes me sad, yet I have been true to the trust, and I die in the thought, I have done my duty, as all have before me. It is years since a stranger's foot has trod these halls, soon perhaps to be desecrated by many such; for strangers will wholly occupy, or neglect, this grand old pile, which will soon crumble, topple, and be forgotten in time.

The last line of nobles were called Rheinbergs,—a real princely race. There were only two brothers left. One was tall and stately, dark and swarthy as a Moor,—with high-arched nose, fierce flaming eyes, a wealth of raven curls; a bold, broad, square, high forehead; a strong, square chin; and an arm of steel; with a soul to dare, and a mind to aspire.

He was proud of carriage, and had a step like a God. His voice had a hard metallic ring in it of high command, short and stern.

His whole manner was imposing and grand. He was the best rider and athlete in the whole country; a man who dared all things, despised competition, and laughed at fear; yet he was beautiful, though of a dark and repellant cast of beauty.

All feared him instinctively; none loved him; 'twas awe that inspired all who approached him.

Even in the day time, when mounted on his
black charger, there was a strange, fierce look
about him, that made men tremble. He said
but little, and his voice was doom.

His brother was a strange, almost a marvel-
ous contrast to him; short of stature, rather
stout of limb, almost portly in his bearing, fair
as the day, with the sweetest heavenly blue eye
ever seen,—a man with a free and open coun-
tenance, with ruddy, full, and laughing lips,
that freely showed the teeth at every smile,
straight Grecian nose, a beautiful arched forehead, with a head full of clustering golden
curls,—a man born for love, homage, and admiration,—with an open hand, an open heart, an
open mind, and an open soul.

He was of a very kind and gentle nature,
sunny as the day, loved by his dependents,
always with a smile for all he met, a jovial
talker, a free liver, and urbane, courteous, and
hospitable, to all.

The elder was rarely willing to receive visitors; yet the younger often coaxed his brother to let him have sway. Then he opened the castle halls to all around him.

Though vastly different, they seemed to almost idolize each other; and Rudolph, the elder, would smile at some merry antic of Frank, the younger. Yet he seldom smiled.

There was a very distant cousin that had been left by will to the care of these brothers, —a young maiden, beautiful as earth could mould.

Ida was her name, a being of a rare and pensive loveliness, soft as the dews of morning; yet of a dark olive hue, with rare and luxuriant tresses of raven blackness. She was tall, and exquisitely formed, with large gazelle eyes, of a strange, dreamy loveliness. She was exceedingly gentle and attractive,—so beautiful that to look upon her was to love her.

She became the rage for miles around; and every noble aspired to her hand. At first Rudolph scarcely noticed her; and it was seen that when Frank approached, the hue heightened on her cheek, and her form trembled; yet Frank had never spoken a word of love, though all could see it in his lingering gaze, the hot flush upon his cheek, and the wonderful kindness and attention which he showed her.

His very look doted on her; and he worshipped with a fond and rare idolatry, as if she was a very saint from heaven. This was apparent to all, even to strangers.

By degrees, Rudolph's manner changed to all who paid her any extra attention. He showered dark and lowering looks; sometimes he even scowled; a strange, bitter smile, wreathed his lips; his whole nature changed; his looks became sullen and clouded; and he often whispered strangely to himself.

One day Ida was weeping convulsively. Frank came suddenly in. The sight astounded him. He was breathless; he was speechless. Suddenly he clenched his hand like steel, and his form trembled with a terrible indignation. He strode up and down like a caged tiger; then, more calm, asked Ida the cause of her sorrow.

She only answered with more weeping, while Frank was in an ecstasy of agony. By piece-meal he learned, that, that very day, Rudolph had asked her hand. In fear and trembling, she told him she could not love him as a wife should love her liege lord.

He became black as midnight, grasped her arm as in a vise, and, with a terrible menace, said,—

"Beware no other, then, asks your hand! By the God of Heaven, I'll crush him as I do this!"—suddenly hurling a chair in fragments upon the floor, and fiercely strode away.

Frank soothed with his own tears this frightened girl, and then strode hastily out.

A groom overheard them in the forest, and told my sire,—yet dared not, for very fear, let it go farther.

"Shame on you, Rudolph, thus to insult our ward! Where is your manhood? Ay, look not so menacing; I fear thee not! The proud blood of our fathers is in my veins as well as in yours, though thou art the elder. Go and see Ida, and make thy excuses to her; or, by my good sword, thou art henceforth no brother of mine!"

"Beware!" Rudolph hissed from his teeth, like the whisper of some deadly snake; "beware thou interferest not between her and me! She shall be mine; or, by high heaven, she shall be a corse!"

"Art thou mad, by brother? Is thy manhood gone?"

"Begone!" said Rudolph. "Thy sight will make me a fratricide! Begone! or, in my agony, I'll do a deed I'll repent of!"

His eyes were terribly inflamed and blood-shot; yet, with such a look of agony and horror blended, it almost made Frank pity him.

Suddenly Rudolph wheeled and rode off, deigning to speak no further,—while a strange, heavy foreboding, filled Frank's soul.

Rudolph was a changed man from that hour. A doom seemed to hang over him; a strange laugh came from his lips; and he often looked upon Frank with a maniac gleam in his sombre eyes.

Whole nights he was seen riding fiercely through the country. All shuddered as he met them, and gave him wide way. A spell seemed to fall upon the castle. The company became fewer and fewer, till at last the castle seemed neglected.

Rudolph watched, with silent, furtive gleam, his brother and Ida together. As she smiled upon Frank, his arm always seemed to clutch the hilt of the poniard which he carried in his bosom; and you could almost hear the grating of his teeth together. All saw the murderous smile flashing in his eyes, yet dared not even hint of it.

He became like a dark statue, and rarely spoke. He stalked through his ancient halls like a lost demon, on whose brow no more a smile was ever seen. Hours, weeks, and months, he would roam far and wide, and come back gaunt and haggard.

His flesh forsook him; and he looked, in time, like a black spectre. The strange, fierce, hard look, in his eyes, deepened; and a fixed, stony stare, of some strange and awful purpose, dwelt there. No one dared even to look at him, as there was something terrible and awful in his gaze.

Frank and Ida were incessantly together when Rudolph was absent; but were very careful of showing too much love in his presence.

Of late, when he did see them together, he laughed sardonically, and hurried quickly away, as though the sight was all the fire of hell to his inflamed vision.

He became almost a skeleton: and, though all pitied him, none dared soothe,—not even Frank.

A strange, unnatural fear, possessed all; and friends—even strangers—began to look upon the castle as haunted.

Every one, far and near, shunned this dark, gloomy abode; and many, in whispers, told what would be the ending.

All felt that some terrible tragedy hung like a spell of Fate over this doomed race.

Alas! it swiftly came.

On Rudolph's face was stamped, as if by fire, the spirit of vengeance!—a look of death! —a deep, concentrated, demoniac hate, too awful and horrible for breath! It seemed as if some demon from the lower world had usurped his form, and reigned within!

Rudolph had been absent for months; and Ida and Frank were dreaming in a heaven of love,—a love that forgot all things in its sweet delirium.

It was toward evening on a fearful stormy day. The rain poured down in torrents; the thunders crashed through the forests; the lightning pierced the gloom in a blaze of vivid fire. It struck often around this old mountain home.

Frank was sitting on that fatal chair. Ida, on a cushion near, was reclining at his feet, with looks of unutterable love dilating her rapt eye.

Frank was just stooping to toy with her raven locks, when suddenly the door was thrown open.

Rudolph saw all at a glance. The sight maddened him; and, with a howl like a maniac, with the spring of doom, he made one bound, drew like lightning his poniard from his breast, and struck again and again the glittering steel into his brother's blood.

All his life seemed concentrated in those blows; for when the bloody scene was over, he fell back in death.

Ida sprang convulsively on Frank's murdered body, and shrieked, "Oh, Frank! oh, Frank!" with a look of frozen horror; and, when she was taken from him, reason had fled.

Life henceforth to her was a blank. The race was ended; and, with love and fidelity, my fathers swore to guard this castle while one remained.

From that fatal hour the home became a haunted castle, shunned as Fate.

I thanked the old woman for her kindness; and, as I rode away, a sad and musing man, when I entered the forest a sardonic laugh seemed to fill my ears, as if they were demon-haunted.

PART II.

FABLES.

FABLES.

THE ROSE AND THE LILY.

NEAR together, in a beautiful garden, dwelt a ROSE and a Lily, who often disputed with each other as to which possessed the loveliest charms.

The LILY one day being vexed, thus harshly upbraided the ROSE:—

"You think yourself beautiful, no doubt, with your round, red, fat face, and your straggling, thick, bushy body, full of vile prickles! Oh, what a dumpy! You are not worthy to compare with my tall, elegant figure, and a face so pale and snowy beautiful!"

Whereupon the ROSE pouted with her ruddy lips, and thus answered in retort:—

"I would not be a bean-pole, with a milk-and-water face stuck on it, just like a figure at mast-head! And as for my thorns, I thank the stars that I have some protection to keep my beauty from being snatched away, whereas any fool that comes along can easily bear you off. Then where is your elegance, your snowy beauty, and the fine lady airs you give yourself?"

Just then, as the ROSE stopped speaking, a spruce miss tripped along; and, with a wanton carelessness, stripped the LILY of its lovely flower; and, leaning over to pluck the ROSE, snatched a thorn. Piqued with the pain, she murmured, "It was not worth the plucking!" and so left it alone in its glory. Whereupon the Rose lifted up her tiny voice exultingly, and clapped her hands in glee.

Her triumph was short-lived; for a fierce wind sweeping over the garden struck her blossoms, and they were scattered upon the gale.

Moral.—So fall Vanity and Pride.

THE PEARL AND THE DIAMOND.

FAIR lady and gallant gentleman, upon a ship at sea, were discussing the merits of a beautiful diamond, when suddenly it dropped into the water, disturbing the repose of a lovely PEARL, sleeping beneath the ocean depths.

Angry at this sudden interruption of her rest, the PEARL thus upbraided the DIAMOND:

"Why did you not stay upon the earth, where such glittering gewgaws as you belong? Do you think to outrival me here in my ocean home! There are millions of sea waves, that, in their sparkling light, can match you in their brilliancy! Do you think to be Queen amid these dancing diamonds of the deep? You who are lifeless, except when the sun lends you his beams. Then, in borrowed glory, you glitter with false lustre, and shower radiance around you, as if it were all your own. Go back to earth again! Here the gay swimmers of the deep can match you, with their network of gold and silver lacings!"

The DIAMOND, with flashing eyes, thus retorted:—

"Not desire, but accident, makes me your unwilling guest. If I am queen of jewels, upon the earth, down in your liquid home I expect not homage from so dull and opaque a thing as yourself. The waves may dash around you forever, and never make your features bright and clear! Your round body, even with the sun's rays flashing full upon it, would never emit a spark of fire! Clouded and dim, your eye has no lustre; and it is well that the sparkling waters hide you beneath their waves. I dwell in the palace, amid the halls of revelry and life. I dance on the brow of beauty. I zone like a girdle of sparkling fire a fair lady's form. And even Love itself has chosen me as the fairest gift to adorn the tapering finger—the pure pledge of a future marriage."

The PEARL thus answered:—

"Do you boast, so enamored are you of your charms? Know that I am a rover amid the coral bowers of the deep; and I listen to the mermaid's song, as she chants soft lullabys in the twilight eve. I listen to the rushing sound of the mighty whale, as he plunges amid the billows. Not out of the earth, gloomy and dark, did I spring forth; not, as you were, from the clods, and striving to outvie the sunlight of heaven, which gives you all your charms. I was born amid the ocean's azure depths, and cradled to slumber by their rocking waters; and, when I die, the ocean waves will forever dirge o'er my remains a sad requiem in their endless play.

Moral.—Each one conceits their charm the loveliest of earth.

NIGHT AND DAY.

A DISPUTE, AND AN APPEAL TO THE SUN.

DAY IS FAIR, VITAL, FEMININE.—NIGHT IS DARK, MASCULINE.

JUST as DAY was retiring, and had put on her nightcap for a quiet sleep, NIGHT approached her, and thus jocularly spoke:—

"Aha, lady fair! Are you tired of the sun's bright glances, that thus early you enroll beneath my banner? Get under my wing, fair lady; and sweet dreams to thee till morning!"

DAY said:—

"Aha, you sly rogue! Would you have me stay to flirt with you, when my gallant lover the Sun has sunk to rest? When the Sun retires within his palace my work is done, and yours begins. We both are servitors of the golden Sun. I watch the working world after the Stars have gone to rest; thou watchest the sleeping earth when the stars break from their slumber."

Night answered:—

"But mine is the most gallant task! For when do lovers walk, if not in the twilight eve, when my form appears in dusky shadow? —and, stretching my mystic wing o'er all things, they are veiled as in a shroud?

"But my dark azure bowers are laden with golden fruit, beneath which confiding lovers sing the song of love, and steal each other's hearts away. You, oh Day! are a cold, chaste Christian, and only have one lover, the gallant Sun! How cold and solitary in your lonely state!

"But not only does the Moon, the Queen of my soul, wave her silvery plumes o'er my dusky brow, with a soft, confiding gaze; but myriad stars, each with a beauty of its own, bend their bright glances upon me, whispering in their midnight vigils songs of love and joy.

"My dusky form is robed in such bewildering beauty, and sparkling with such celestial fires, that I almost rival the pomp and glory of the Sun himself."

Day retorted:—

"Dost thou compare thy dusky Mohammedan paradise, where thou languishest the hours away in fondling dalliance, with the voluptuous houris of the heavens, with the constant love of the great Sun, whose fiery love o'erwhelms me with his splendor, and takes my heart by storm?

"What are the few sparkles on your robe of night compared to the blaze of fires that light up my gay empire? I never veil my beauty in a dusky mantle, half ashamed to be seen; but when the SUN salutes me, I return the kiss before all the world.

"Behold my glory! Life is everywhere. List the busy hum of toil! The world of man, cheered by my bright presence, ransacks earth, water, and air, piling up the stored wonders of science, art, and manufactures."

Thus they continually disputed with each other; which the SUN overhearing, they appealed to him to decide.

The SUN thus addressed them:—

"My children: Do not argue! What would man's life and health, strength and beauty, be, if thou, oh NIGHT! did not fan him with thy wing to slumber, giving rest to the exhausted muscles, nerves, and blood?

"Would not the flowers and leaves wither, if thou, oh NIGHT! did not bedew them with thy gentle tears, bathing their parched brows

from the starry fountain, which soothes their
fever, and renews their beauty when the morn
appears?

"With thee, oh NIGHT, comes rest to all,—a
balm to toil. When thou appearest, thy twin
sister, SLEEP, also appears, dividing thy dark
empire with her.

"Oh, NIGHT! What a wild train moves
around thy throne! Ghosts, visions, dreams,
nightmares, fairies, and sprites,—all the dim
shadows of an unreal world!—and though thy
reign seems like death, there is strange magic
in it.

"All moving life now becomes silent as the
grave, and the Angel of Death seems holding
reign; and naught is heard but the music of
the airy harps that breathe from the lips of
the sleeping Earth.

"Oh, DAY! Do not taunt thy dusky friend!
Though she is black as an Ethiop, jewels rare
deck her form! And thou, oh NIGHT! do not

deride the DAY! What would the world be without her, but one vast solitude? Gaze upon the DAY's bright eye, when at morn she looks upon the earth! See a world of stars upon every leaf and flower!—even vying with your loves, oh NIGHT!

"List the melody of birds! Nature, warmed by the sunshine, dances o'er the earth in a million charms. The earth feels the sun's warm kisses; the harvest grows; fruits ripen; man exults in toil; and all the tribes of earth go to their allotted tasks.

"A busy world moves on during the hours, till they fall into thy embrace, oh, NIGHT! and are lost in dreams and sleep.

"My darlings! Each has a beauty, witchery, and grandeur of her own! God made both DAY and NIGHT. He made DAY to glitter, to dazzle, to toil. He made NIGHT to soothe, to rest.

"Day is the spirit of motion. Night is the spirit of sleep.

"Each travels o'er the years, hand in hand, to that home where all is light.

"Ye are co-equal, both in your sweetness and in your power, and with myself. We are God's handmaidens to wait on man.

Moral.—Each in his sphere is great.

THE FOX AND THE GOOSE.

FOX one day came to a pond to drink; and, looking around, espied a goose calmly floating on the water.

"Good morning!" said the Fox. "Friend, you look charming to-day! Come near, and shake hands with me! Let us be warm friends!"

"I am afraid," said the Goose, "that you will be too friendly!—entirely too warm! Your embrace will be too earnest! Aha! old Fox, we know you!—with your soft flatteries to catch silly geese with; but I am an old Goose, and up to your tricks! If I am charming,

take a good look at me, as I sail around the
pond. We can converse as well, and enjoy as
nice a tete-a-tete; and you know it is safer, too.
Ah, ha! Mr. Fox, I've got you there!"

And the Goose chuckled.

The Fox retorted:—

"Oh, you suspicious fool! What are you
afraid of? I'll not harm you! I'm lonely
this morning; and I would be sociable,—that's
all! Come, now, don't keep aloof, like a her-
mit; but approach, and be more friendly. I
would salute you! In truth, I am enamored
of your beauty! Indeed, you are a plump darling! You are the fairest creature I've seen
this many a day! Indeed, I am really charmed!
I am in raptures!"

The Goose answered that she was not to be
caught by a sly, cozening old Fox.

"I've seen you before! I know you of old!
You have been the talk of the country this
many a day! Your reputation is poor, indeed!

We have all been told to beware of you! Ah, ha! Mr. Fox, I'm sorry I can't return your very sweet, highly spiced, and very flattering compliments! To tell the truth, I think you are a sly old rogue!—a cozening rascal!—a fawning sneak!—full of silly lies and soft speeches, to catch simpletons with. I am too old a Goose to be caught with chaff!"

The Fox, madly indignant, burst out:—

"You superannuated, cowardly wretch! You old waddling, clumsy, long-necked fool! It is well you are out of reach, or else I would twist your neck for your insolence! But I'll bide my time! I'll catch you yet! A Fox is a match for a Goose any day!"

The Goose retorted:—

"I guess the grapes are sour!"

Moral.—Flattery don't always succeed.

THE CAT AND THE MOUSE.

PUSS once on a time espied a little MOUSE entering his hole, and softly stole up to him.

The MOUSE heard the noise, and turned round to see what was the matter.

Puss.—Ah, ha! my little love! Come out, and let us have a romp together! You little sleek darling! We'll have a glorious play! Come out, and see if you can't catch me! We'll wager who will win; and, if you beat, I have a nice bit of cheese to give you! Come!

The Mouse hesitated,—Puss was so soft, so kind, so gentle,—and he half advanced, and half retreated.

Puss.—Why, you dear little sly thing! How modest you are!—how fearful! Come, I only want to play! I'll not harm you! I only want a romp, as I am sure you can't catch me! Try, do!—that's a little darling!—and if you do, the cheese is yours!

The Mouse, thus tempted, suddenly bounded out; and Puss, first in sport, round and round chased him in a circle,—leaped here, leaped there, and gently rapped him on the nose.

The Mouse, alarmed, took fright, and suddenly darted for his hole.

"No, you don't!" says Puss, seizing him at once. "You are too nice a morsel for my dinner, to let you go! I'll put you in my larder!"

No sooner said than done; and this was the last of the little Mouse.

Moral.— Don't trust strangers, however specious.

LIGHT AND SHADOW.

LIGHT.

YOU are always in my way! I never send my sunbeams o'er the earth, but you must follow my footsteps! You pursue me like a hound upon the scent!—like an echo reverberating to an echo! You are my pest!—the daily nightmare to dim my splendor! I can not move, or breathe, or think, but you must follow after! Why do you thus thrust your dark face into the sunlight of my home? Am I never to be rid of you?

SHADOW.

Why, you selfish whiner! Why should you possess all the earth? Did God make the light only? In your conceit, you think all admire you alone!

I tell you, man delights in my shade, when you, in your fierce heats, would consume him! He often longs for me; and, if you are a servitor of his pleasures, so God made me also to please him. If in winter he most delights in you, in summer I am sure I am the favorite,—so do not always growl at me; but hand in hand divide the joys of earth,—you in your sphere, I in mine.

But I deny that I dim your splendor, you short-sighted one! I only make your glory appear the brighter! In your passion, you overlook how great the contrast is between us. That contrast redounds to your honor!

It is the dark setting that makes the diamond more radiant.

So I am your friend,—an humble one, it is true,—but ever will I follow thee. God has made it so; and thank Him for the favor. He has bestowed; so do not destroy the little He has given me. The humblest as well as the greatest are entitled by the grace of God to the happiness their respective spheres contain. In your greatness, then, don't despise the lowly shade, for it is but a foil to your brightness. So ignorance is a foil to knowledge, vice to virtue, life to death. The lesser only adds to the honor of the greater: it can not detract.

MORAL.—Selfishness claims all.

THE DOG AND THE CAT.

SAVAGE Dog once treed a Cat. Poor Puss, looking down, thus questioned him:—

"Why do you always pursue me? Why do you wish to harm me? I never trouble you! Do let me go! You can not eat me! What good, then, thus to torment me?"

DOG.

Don't you torment the little mice?—tease them till they are half dead with fright?—then eat them? When you get together, don't you always quarrel, and make the fur fly?—make

the night hideous, and disturb my sleep? My
master often curses your midnight caterwaul-
ings, that sound like the orgies of demons!

PUSS.

I know I eat the mice and rats, for they
are my natural food; and God ordained it so.
But don't you eat the tender lamb? Are you,
then, any more humane than I am? I know
we sometimes disturb the night; but don't you,
also? Hear how you howl!—how you bark!
—and prolong your whine till old Sleep himself awakes to see what is the matter! Don't
you fight when you meet, and tear and shake
each other like two devils in a fury? But we
poor cats don't disturb you! We never pursue
you! Why, then, are you so cruel?

DOG.

So, ho! What a preacher you have become!
What a petitioner! Quite a lawyer! But it
don't go down with me! You know you hate
me in your heart!—that it is not good will

you bear me, but only fear! If you were the
stronger, oh, how soon you would destroy me!
All your fine thoughts would then be nothing!
Come down! You are mine! I hate you! I
know I am cruel! Can you expect any thing
better of a Dog? I have no religion, like a
man!—no conscience, no hereafter, no Bible!
I am only a brute!—untaught! So come
down, or else I'll wait till you do!

PUSS.

If that is the case, I'll come down while I
am still fresh and strong; but you have not
got me yet! I'll see if my agility can't dodge
your brutality. If I am not strong, I am light
and supple, quick and active, and these qualities
may yet overmatch your strength.

DOG.

Come down, and make the trial; and success
to the winner.

MORAL.—Agility often overmatches mere
brute strength.

THE WIND AND THE AIR.

AIR.

DO let me have a little peace! I never get to rest, but you must blow upon me! But what can we expect of a fickle wind? Can't you be quiet? Go among the clouds, and set them in a whirl! I am weary, so let me rest.

WIND.

Rest, indeed! You lazy child! If I did not stir you up now and then, you would grow stagnant, diseased, and die! Thank Heaven I put on the lash betimes, to keep you stirring!

I drive the mildew from your brow!—the slime from your fountains!—the miasma from your home!

Why, you would rust unto death, did I not whirl my eddies around you, and galop in the whirlwind! I am not born for your pleasure only, but as a servitor for man's enjoyment.

When the fierce rains descend, how he longs for the drying winds! When the clouds of insects come, how he longs for the breeze! It rouses the stagnant blood, it drives away fever, and fills the earth with freshness and health, bringing roses to cheek and lip, and sending the warm current bounding within.

I am your family doctor, Miss AIR, and dose you with such wholesome drugs, they keep you ever young and fair. You must admit I am very gentle at times,—soft as down, or a floating gossamer. So serene is my visit, that I scarcely stir the sunbeam, whose golden lip salutes thine own!

I know that when you spend too much time sporting with the sunbeams, and lie in voluptuous dreams, dissolved in amorous fire, that I often rudely give you a shock, and send you whirling to your senses. 'Tis better thus, than to lie idly in love's enervating arms!

AIR.

Indeed, you are often very rough!—only half civil, and sound so fierce a trumpet in my ear that you almost split my drum! If I was not insured in heaven, and wind-proof, long ere now I were dumb for ever!

WIND.

Come, come! A truce to your chidings! Let us be friends! Let my gentle wooings make amends for my fierce passions! If at times I am all love itself, sueing with the sweetest smiles and most loving cadences, at times I play the churl,—the master.

Do I not waft to your nostrils the scents of all the flowers? I attend upon the months,

To them I first am bound; and if I oft salute thee sweetly in the soft, balmy, fragrant winds of summer, I must howl in the opening spring! I can not always tune my trumpet to one note, but I must pitch my changes to suit the seasons. If I play the organ in winter, I can play the flute in summer! You know, Miss AIR, I have made you an accomplished performer,— the wonder and the delight of the world!

Oh, how beautifully sweet is your æolian harp!—and how deliciously sighing is your wooing moans through the green pines!

AIR.

I know I have had a prolonged and most severe training; for I can play all tunes, from the roar of the toppling avalanche, the shriek of the whirlwind, to the softest notes of an unclouded summer eve, when my dulcet notes are like a dying swan's, or like the dying whisper of melody itself.

You must own I was an apt scholar. So apt, indeed, that few could tell the scholar from the tutor!

WIND.

Well, well! Now that we are friends again, I own that, like twins, we play the same tunes, and are strung on the same key; and if we sing in unison, let our hearts be harmonious. So, good day.

MORAL.—The business and the man who pursues it often become alike.

THE BUTTERFLY AND THE ANTS

BEAUTIFUL Butterfly alighted one day near an ant-hill; and, looking at their bodies loaded with all kinds of stores for their winter use, broke out into a gay laugh, and exclaimed:—

"Why, you poor drudges! You slow pack-horses! How you toil! Poor fellows! Look at me! See how I flit from flower to flower, sipping their sweets! Look at my wing of gold! O'er all the earth I sail, floating on the airy billows; and my pinions, like sails, waft me on. Don't you wish you could leave your toil, and roam with me from tree to tree, and climb the hill-tops, and look afar? You never see aught! Toil! toil! 'Tis your life!—your breath!—your dower!

"My life is a round of pleasure!—a gay holiday!—a dancing whirl!—here and there, and everywhere! Behold our plumage! Like floating rainbows, we sail on the hours, giddy with delights! Come, you poor little ants! Come with me, and let me tuck you beneath my wings, and let us have a sail together. We'll roam o'er all the flowers, and surfeit you with sweets. We will alight on the tree-tops; and beneath the green shade we'll sing the time away. Come!"

THE ANTS.

No, no! Miss BUTTERFLY, we can not spare the time! Winter is coming, and we must provide against the cold. We are but humble toilers, and don't possess your gaudy plumage —your rainbow hues. We can not float upon the air, and sail upon the winds. Our toil is sweet; and, after our day's labor, how nicely we rest! We have no time to be unhappy, since we are so busy, which brings us sweet content.

When winter comes, beneath the earth we have our dances, our frolics, and our feasts. All winter long 'tis a holiday,—a continual rest. You have so much idle time on your hands, one would think you would weary of it. Besides, how long does your life last? When winter comes, you shrivel with the cold!— your life is ended! Short, short, indeed, vain child of pleasure, is your day! A flit, a sip, a chill, then death!

With all your fine feathers, you are but a grub, after all! Clip your wings, then what are you but a worm? You have crawled many a day upon the earth, as we do now, and burrowed into the dirt! A pair of wings makes you proud, indeed!

We envy you not, short-lived popinjay of a day! Your wealth is not lasting, while ours is prolonged for many a day. It is true we are not gay rovers, as you are,—that we do not keep up such state,—but we are substantial, plain, and sensible; and if we do not enjoy so much, we enjoy it longer.

We fear not the cold! We shrivel not up at the first blast of adversity! With all your fine feathers, we would not exchange with you!

BUTTERFLY.

Well, well, toil on! I am going to have a sail! Look at me, as I spread my wings! Am I not beautiful? See how I dive and whirl! Light as a feather, I careen around the earth! I am the envy of all the insect tribes! I am their queen! Day-day, little ants!

And, with a reckless laugh, the butterfly sailed on.

THE ANTS.

We haven't time to watch your antics! We have work to do of more importance. Go, and waste your time! Winter will soon be here, and the cold will bring you to your senses!

MORAL.— Industry and toil always bring their reward, while a life of pleasure soon fades.

PEACOCK AND CANARY-BIRD.

A LOVELY little golden-winged canary was trolling a carol one fine spring morning, perched on a bar in his cage, when he was suddenly stopped in his song by the haughty sneer of a magnificent PEACOCK, who was just marching by, his feathers spread to the sun, brilliantly lighting up their splendid dazzling colors, glittering like a myriad rainbows coiled together.

As he spoke, he upreared still more lordly his arching neck, as if to send his words into the CANARY's very ears.

PEACOCK.

What a chatterbox you are! It seems to me your tongue is always a-going! I should think you would split your throat with so much singing! Your eternal babbling almost deafens me! It pierces me to the very marrow! I wonder what folks see in your little noisy body, so much to admire!

Why, you are no bigger than a man's thumb, yet you roar as loudly as a March blast! You affright the very air with your songs, your trills, your carols, your catches, and your piercing shrieks! For my part, I wish you would be silent when I pass along! I am tired of your eternal warbling!

CANARY.

Why, Mr. Fuss-and-feathers! — Mr. Strut! Do you envy me my few snatches of song? Don't you have the stroll of the whole place? Are you not the fine gentleman amongst the feathered tribes? Are you not satisfied with your magnificent trail, glistening like colored jewels in the sun's rays,—a natural kaleidoscope, for all to gaze at and admire?

I know I am only a wee thing; but don't you know the most valuable goods are done up in the smallest parcel? I don't wonder you envy me my voice; for when you open your mouth, it is only "e-ow! e-ow!"

You are made only for display! Be content, and spread your feathers! Uprear your stately neck, and proudly strut! All the world will gaze! You are a walking jewel, rainbow-gemmed, made for the eye alone! Admiration is your dower, but no love!

I am only a hop-o'-my-thumb, but sweet song is my dower, and the love of all belongs to me. I am the children's pet, who stroke me softly, call me little love, and bid me sing my sweetest notes.

You are free to wander. It matters not whether you are lost or no. You are not of

much account! But I am prized so highly
that they put me in a gilded cage. I am
waited on, as upon a king! Don't you see I
live in royal state? They fear to lose me!
They'd miss my songs, and my cheering salute
at early morn.

PEACOCK.

Well, sing on! I suppose you will! It is,
as you say, your dower; but it don't change
my mind. I can not see any use in keeping
such a plain, insignificant-looking thing. Why,
you almost drown the wind in your shrieking!
But I'll march on, as I have lost caste already
in condescending to notice you so long! The
world will think you are one of my set! It
will spoil the prestige I have gained as an
exclusive,—the *bon ton* of the feathered aristocracy!

CANARY.

Your fine airs give me no concern! The
truly gentle most delight in me! Let vulgar

gazers follow after your train! They receive only barren honors, and soon weary of your charms, whilst I am ever welcome, and my delicious music is a passport to all hearts!

I am the people's pet, and I sit by the hearthstone of the peasant as well as by the throne of the king! I sing as sweetly for the poor forsaken outcast as I do for one showered with fortune's favors. With all my gifts, I am modest, humble, and content. I crave not honors, admiration, or respect; but all I ask is Love and Friendship; and all the world gives me these in return for my sweet warblings.

PEACOCK.

You have wondrous conceit of your mental charms, for so small a body! It is well so fine a spirit was put into so small a compass. If it owned my lordly presence, the world were too small for your dwelling-place! You would wish the great sun itself for a home!

Your voice would outroar the ocean blast, the whirlwind's shriek, or the earthquake's rumble!

It is well you are born so insignificant and powerless! They cage you up to keep you, and why? Because you are so inconstant!—so unsteady! You are a giddy flirt! To-day, come here! To-morrow, go there! No place or station could keep you long!

So a prisoner of state you'll always be!—a singing slave to wait on lordly man! I am content to stay at home; or, if I do wander, it is only a little visit, and I soon return.

CANARY.

It is not your worth, but worthlessness, that makes you free! It matters little if you did wander, and ne'er returned. No love follows your absent footsteps; but I am a golden gift, to be treasured in a wire casket! Man fears to lose me! I can not easily be replaced!

I win the heart; and my bonds are made with the hands of love, not hate! I am happy, and grateful for man's favors; and I sing my sweetest notes to repay him for all his care.

PEACOCK.

Heigho! What conceit! What self-applause! What honors you take to yourself! What boasting! I'll march on, or else, in your great-ness, you'll steal my train! At least, if songs could do it, no doubt it would be yours!

CANARY.

I would not carry such a load for all the world! No, thank you! I am light and active, and that is enough for me. You are welcome to your fine feathers; but don't brag too loud, or else I'll see you some fine day in a lady's chamber, brushing the cobwebs from the wall! Then you'll be of use and profit; but now you are but a jack-a-dandy for fools to gape at, and wise men to wonder at your airs!

PEACOCK.

I'll go, or else you'll be hoarse with so much talking; and with your singing, 'twill spoil your voice! Then you are fit only for the cat! He'll be your best friend! You'll be his little love! And, in most delicious morsels, he'll dissect you; and find in you only a common bird, after all!—the most insignificant of dishes!—only a bite!

MORAL.—Real merit often belongs to the plainest looking.

WINTER AND SPRING.

NE season, WINTER, as he retired for the year, saluted the coming SPRING with so fierce a welcome that SPRING leaped up in much surprise, and, indignant, thus spoke:—

"So, ho! old Jack! What is the matter with you, this year? Have you been napping for months, and just waked up to have a growl? I thought you had roared enough, and had settled down for a nice nap; or else be sure I would not have disturbed you so soon! To tell the truth, you saluted me in so loud a key, as almost made me start for home again, till I was sure you were really gone.

OLD JACK.

None of your airs, Miss SPRING! I like not your affected surprise,—your apologetic speeches! I know you always steal a *March* upon me, when you can. You like to catch me napping, so that you can place your heaters around me to melt me to tears, and so make me a useful servant during your three months' reign.

You know very well, when March comes I get consumptive, and a warm spring sun soon collapses me into water! You had better retire for the present. To-day I am wide awake; and defy you, with all your warm embraces, and your insinuating address. I am old Jack still, with ice and sleet, hail and snow.

SPRING.

I ask your pardon, Jack, for thus disturbing you so early. Really, I was in haste to tread upon your toes! I thought I must be up betimes, and prepare the soil for various grains, beautiful flowers, and most delicious vegetables.

JACK FROST.

Don't presume too soon, this year, you soft coquette; or else I'll nip all your buds, and destroy your fruit! I'm in no humor for any jokes this month! Approach me gently, or else you'll get so fierce a blast 'twill spoil your new wedding-dress, and ruin your prospects all the season!

SPRING.

I'll take care next time, Jack, to keep out of your way. You're as rough as an old bear, sometimes; and 'tis well to get out of your clutches! But you presume somewhat. I tell you that!

It is time you disappeared! All are tired of seeing you usurp so long a time all the hours. I leave you a week to pack up, bag and baggage. Then I'll come with such force and power, that if in honor you'll not depart, we'll tumble you out, pell mell!

JACK FROST.

I care not. Do as you like best. Leave me, now. Let me blow my trump once more, and send the snowflakes dancing o'er the earth, and have a jubilee. Then off I'll go, and leave the earth to your smiles and soft caresses. No doubt you'll coax out of the earth a million treasures, which will adorn your robe of state, and make you for a time Queen.

MORAL.—Don't be too quick to step into another person's shoes.

THE BEAR AND THE BEES.

BLACK bear was caught stealing the hive from the hollow trunk of an old tree, by some bees just returning with a fresh supply of honey.

BEES.

Ah, ha! you lazy rascal! You great lubberly fellow! Ain't you ashamed thus to steal a march upon us, and rob us of all our summer's toil?

You have the free range of the woods, and can get plenty of roots, nuts, and other stores. We never rob you of your share of necessaries.

Ain't you sly, to watch us go, and then come and take all in a moment,—the whole family supply for winter's use?

The BEAR half hung his head, mortified at being caught in the act; and half growled sullenly, as if in doubt whether to fight it out, or steal away in shame.

But the bees gathering around him, the fresh smell of new honey stole into his nostrils, and stimulated him suddenly to make a dash for the hive, which he had relinquished on their appearance.

The comb fell scattered upon the ground, and the bear's nose was poked into the delicious sweets, when a fierce attack of the bees started him into a leap, while a thousand needles pierced him to the quick.

"You old rascal!" cried the bees, "how do you like that? Run for your life, or we'll let another squadron of pikes upon you!"

Over and over, roaring and growling, he tumbled upon the ground,—kicking and leaping with the agony, but not willing to leave the hive.

A second and a third attack, more fierce than ever, sent him flying, with the whole swarm after him. Again and again they let fly their darts, till he was stuck all over with javelins. Then, howling and panting, half dead upon the ground he lay exhausted,—his foes, spent also with the fierce fight, gazing sternly on.

BEES.

See, you old thief, the reward for your rascality! You thought, because we were small and insignificant, you could do as you pleased, and appropriate your neighbor's goods as your own, relying upon your great bulk and shaggy hide. But remember, all can fight, when they fight for home, food, and shelter.

We hope it will be a warning to you, in the future, to mend your ways, and mind your own business! Promise never to trouble us again, and we'll leave you to penitence and reflection.

The bear sullenly growled assent, and rubbed his sides wofully, to ease the pain. The bees, triumphant, flew away, and with energy started a new hive.

MORAL.—In union there is strength.

SUN AND SNOW.

SNOW.

IS it not a shame, when I have just arranged my robes, and softly spread my mantle o'er the earth, and beautifully concealed the naked form of Winter, in his ermine dress of state, and hid with fleecy down all the barrenness of Winter, with his grimness and deformity, and tasseled the gray limbs in feathery silver, and made earth look young and beautiful,—that you must come and spoil all my work; and, with your fiery darts, pierce me to the quick, and uncase me with your beams, and again leave earth desolate and lone? The Harvest Spirit will not thank you for your meddlesome fervor!

SUN.

Why, Miss Snow, you know you are a very superficial observer! You don't expect always to last! You have had a good reign this winter, I guess; and 'tis time you were on the March!

Miss Spring has bid me sweep you into the ocean, with all your fleeces and robes, icicles, and ice-bound jewelry! You have had a good reign, with your piling flakes; and have made the roads impassable, and kept people within doors. In truth, you have heaped up your robes in fantastic piles, in every imaginable position.

You have this winter fairly choked up the earth with your goods, and strewn your parcels with a reckless freedom that now requires restraint! So, now, my time has come!

I have orders to unlace you, and put you to rest till another year. So prepare for your summer nap; for I'll listen to no excuses. Miss SPRING now holds the reins; and you know she is a furious driver! She don't spare the whip!

If you come in her way, she'll overwhelm you with a shower-bath, that will send you shivering into spray! I am bound in honor to melt you, till you become one running stream. Your bound service to old WINTER is now over. You'll have to put off your state, and become a handmaid to the brooks and streams, fill up the springs, and whirl down the watercourses! I will stir up your stagnant blood, and keep you brisk and active.

Your sleep is over! Now you must leap in the torrent, fall in the shower, dash down the cascade, shoot with the avalanche, plunge with the cataract, tumble o'er the fall, and arch in the rainbow.

You'll be full of business, I'll warrant you, and have no time for vain regrets. Your new sphere will be as useful, as beautiful, as your old vocation. Your dancing rills will sparkle in the sun, and your liquid form will wander amid the clouds, when I draw you up from your many fountains, and glow in scenes of wonderful and fantastic beauty,—in piles of silver snow that look like alps of air, in soft spread fleeces of the heavens in flecked vermillion braids, in misty veils of shadowy glory, in a blaze of golden fires that stretch along the horizon's edge, and even in your daring power o'erawe the sun himself, and veil him from mortal eye.

SNOW.

Well, well, melt me into tears! Dissolve my ice palaces! Disperse my feathery pageant! I'll not die amidst the ruins! No! In other forms of beauty I'll appear!

You'll see me mock you some fine summer

morn, as I gem the leaves and flowers in a world of glittering diadems! As you rainbow the foaming cascade, I'll be there mocking your brilliant hues; and where'er you hurl your beams, there you'll find me in myriad forms!

In the soft gentle dews of night you'll behold my presence! In the dancing showers, I'll whirl to the song of the birds, and the music of the whistling winds!

SUN.

I thought you would come to your senses, and forget your former state in the joy and pleasure of your new pastime. Indeed, I'll see you very often; and, in friendly rivalry, we'll robe the earth in surprising splendor.

MORAL.—We often shine in a new sphere as well as we did in the old.

THE MIRROR AND THE BEAUTY.

MIRROR, very elegantly ornamented with gold, hung in a lady's boudoir. It belonged to a belle and beauty; and took offence one day at being used so often, and thus upbraided the beauty:—

You vain, giddy thing! Why do you thus waste the precious hours in so long gazing at yourself? I should think you would weary of your charms! At least I am tired of seeing one alone always! I wish that some other person would use me, if only for a contrast!

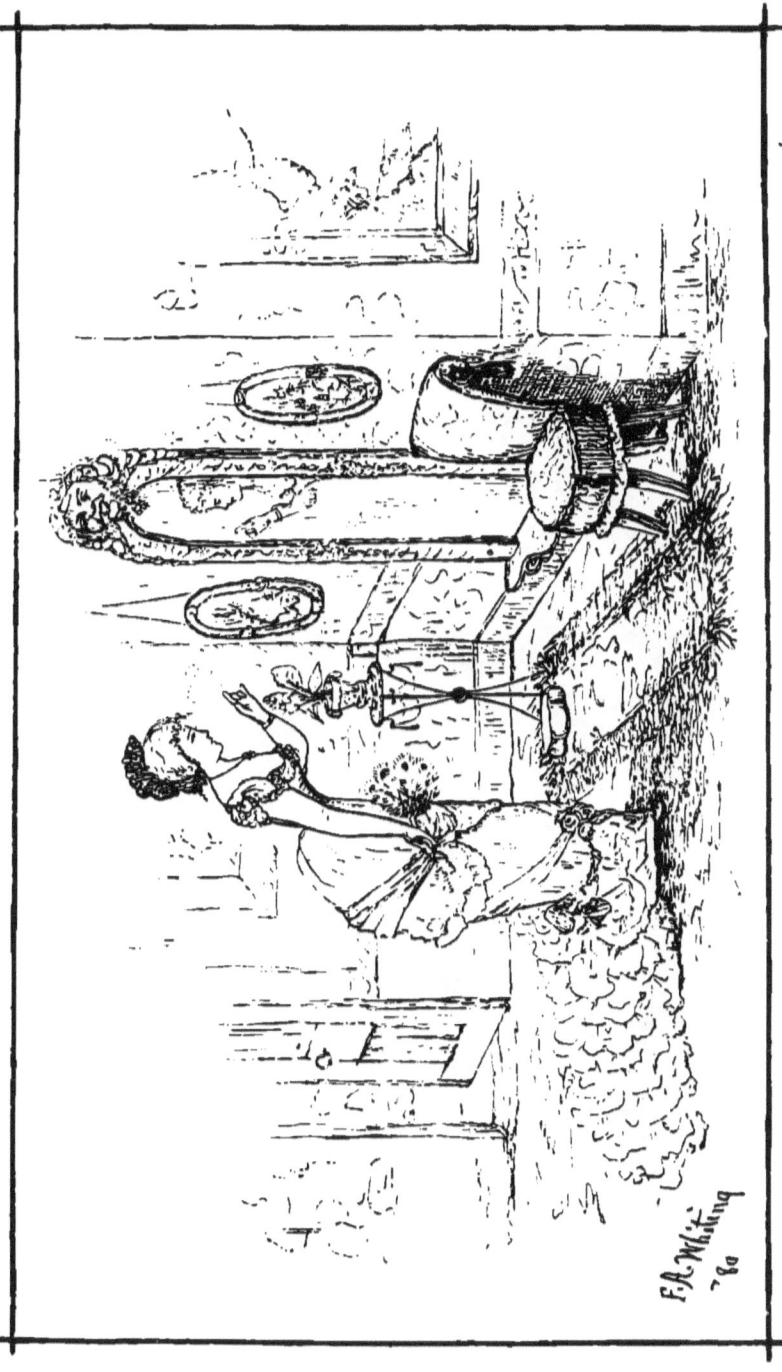

Do you know that age is creeping on you, and all your cosmetics, oils, and powders,—your stays and artificial helps,—will not keep you from wrinkles, cares, and decline?

I see you, day after day, cultivate fine airs, and trick out your body, to catch the eye only! How much better and wiser it would be to spend the hours in providing for the future,—in cultivating those graces which will never fade—a sweet temper, a cultivated mind, a graceful mien, an obliging spirit, and a contented soul! I know I am your bound slave, and will always do your bidding; but I am no flatterer! I can not conceal the ravages of time, since I tell exactly the truth! I can not prevent gray hairs, a sallow skin, an emaciated body, and dull, lusterless eyes! All the arts of the toilet are then only false flatterers that cheat only the foolish!

The BEAUTY, with a disdainful toss of the

head, and a haughty curl of the upper lip, thus poutingly replied:—

Don't fret yourself about the future! I only care for the present! It is enough for me that I am the center of attraction in the ballroom, am the observed beyond all others on the promenade, and am the best ornament of my gay equipage when I roll upon the avenue!

I am the delight of the gentlemen, and the envy of the ladies! How many sigh for the glance of my eye, and a graceful wave of my hand? Are you tired of me gazing so often in your bright face, to see my own reflected there?

How many gallant gentlemen would give a world to be in your place, and see me thus decking my person in all the graces of a fine lady of fashion?

MIRROR.

I wish they would come and see all the airs you give yourself! How much time you waste on mere ornament! What a parlor doll you are! How many tricks you possess to heighten your charms! And with what artificial conceits you deck your person to hide each defect, and make you outparagon the rest of the world!

If they saw you as you really are, your hair would not seem so luxuriant and so glossy beautiful! Your skin would not look like Persia's roses! Your breath would not seem like the lily scent!

The redolent perfumes you throw around you by the skill of science conceal all defects! Well, I suppose you are a human butterfly, and will use your wings till the winter of life overtakes you, and then you'll find yourself only a grub, after all!

BEAUTY.

Why, you cynic, how you rail! Can't you pardon a little vanity in one so lovely as I am?

It is not you, Mr. Mirror, that has discovered my charms. No, indeed! But the world of flatterers, of fawners, the manly trail after my skirts, have told me what I am!

Why do they pursue me? Why sing ever in my praise? Why sigh and write billet-doux? Where'er I go a host of lovers throng around me! They ransack earth, air, and water, to do me honor! I am an angel of light!—the glory of the earth!—the fairest rose of the world's bower!—fashion's fairy sprite!—the brightest jewel of the drawing-room!—a walking grace!—a breathing statue of perfection! —a robed queen of style and art, surpassingly beautiful!

At my beck and nod, a host stand ready to be my slaves! They haunt me as doth the shadow the sunbeam!

Do you wonder, then, that all this homage doth make me think myself a goddess, indeed?

and drives me by all the arts to heighten my beauty, and prolong my sway! Is it not natural? Is it not proper?

MIRROR.

Oh, it is a hollow pomp, after all! It is a deceptive train! They only worship the gloss which surrounds you! Let but disease spoil your beauty, and then see the crowd disappear! Then there will be none so poor as to do you reverence!

They'll fall from you as from a pestilence, and the mirror then will be your only friend! It will strip you of the false lures which veneered your giddy pride, and make you see yourself as you really are!

Let not a rosy cheek, or glossy curl, or dewy eye, deceive you in heightening those charms which soon fade; but rather cultivate those mental graces, those moral virtues, which alone conceal decay, and make it forgotten.

Age without these is a barren state, desolate and lone; but with them, it can yet draw the train which in early youth only follows beauty, wealth, and fashion.

BEAUTY.

Well, indeed, you have preached quite a homily! I forgive the plainness for the truth you express. But, saith the proverb, sufficient unto the day is the evil thereof.

I am not one of your croakers! I don't always think of winter when it is summer! I drink in the soft air! I scent the flowers! I bask in the sunshine, and sip the sweets as they grow around me!

My fair friend, I intend to use you as long as I am young and lovely. It will be time enough to discard you when I am old and ugly! So expect me daily to renew my charms in your bright face, and make myself, if I can, the wonder of the world!

MIRROR.

Well, make old Time your friend as long as you can; for soon he'll strip you of your charms, and repay with scorn all his former love! Adieu!

MORAL.—Physical charms soon fade.

THE CLOUD AND THE SUNBEAM.

SUNBEAM.

OH, thou lazy Cloud!—always floating before my vision! You obscure the view, and dim my brightness! Send on, and let the world gaze upon my beauty. Like a parasite, you always follow me! Am I never to be rid of so unwelcome a guest?

CLOUD.

Don't be too proud of your bright glances, or else I'll veil your beams in a dusky shroud that soon will hide you from view.

Am I a parasite? Do I not wreathe you in floating piles of wondrous beauty? Do I not heap up fleecy pillows for your couch of state? Do I not spangle your robes of light with the changing hues of the dying dolphin?

Do I not spread o'er the heavens, for your adornment, a cashmere mantle, buoyant as the air, tasseled with scattered threads of gold and silver?

Ah, if I am a parasite, I am a useful one, and set off your beams with my floating gossamers, and robe you in royal ermine, imperial purple, or mourning robes, to deck your form when you weep for some star lost in space, whose light has gone out forever!

I acknowledge I hang upon your footsteps, but I am not idle. No; I gather up in the heavens the mists and fogs, and then I spangle the earth with refreshing showers. Ah, then you dance in the glittering drops, and your bright beams look like a mine of diamonds, all resplendent, as if the air held a bridal fete.

I clothe the winter as I fall to earth in the

soft snow-fleece, to warm the young grain and the little seeds of earth, all germs of beauty and of life protecting till the spring. I often veil your fierce heats in the arid summer,—then, oh, how welcome to man! After the torrid drought, when all earth seems scorched, then I gather in my might, and robe the heavens with a midnight pall! Then, look, how I rush to earth, breaking my pent-up heart in the cascade of raindrops,—an avalanche of showers!

How thankful is man for my presence, then! How welcome! With all your brightness, you would be a tame monotony if I did not wreathe you in vermilion dyes, sparkling like the morning; for I surround you with fleeces more beautiful than ever fair lady wore.

SUNBEAM.

Well, well, I was too hasty! My fierce spirit irks at restraint. I can not expect always to have my vision unclouded; but it often stops my view, and I am often forgotten in the royal beauty you array yourself in.

If I am a great ball of fire, you have as wonderful a charm, and often divide my gay empire. Only be a little more careful in your approaches, and not too often dim my vision. You know my power is terrible; and I am merciless when I am aroused.

CLOUD.

A fig for your power! I own not your sway! I obey One greater than you, with all your diamond beauty. I am a royal spy upon your actions. So play no amorous pranks, or be too free with Nature and her beauties; or else I'll come rushing on the winds, driving my chariots with steeds like the ocean foam! You are fixed in the heavens, while I can travel with the whirlwind, sport on the air, and dance merrily in rain and snow, floating in the gray mists of morning, or held in airy Alps piled mountains high.

I laugh at your power, as I am buoyant, light, and gay as a butterfly; and can as easily escape your grasp as does old Time the life of man.

SUNBEAM.

Ah, you are a flimsy, light-headed fop, after all!—a mere floating hanger-on of the hours! A kind of airy fossil of the sky, so lazily breathing as to seem scarcely to exist!

CLOUD.

I acknowledge you often robe me in glory, as you weave your beautiful colors in my floating films; but the gain to your state is greater than the benefit I receive. Do not chide, as we each have our time for usefulness.

Even you, with all your burning pride, will yet sink among the spheres, and be known no more; for when your day comes, the Great Spirit will brush you from space as a cobweb is swept from a wall; but while the universe lasts, my films will float upon the air, as buoyant as at present, as long as the burning spheres exist.

Humble as I am, I have my place in Creation as well as you; and the Great Father smiles equally on both. So be more gentle in your greetings, or else I'll gather in my forces to veil you in misty gray, to make you look like old Time; and so dim will you show as to appear scarcely greater than a rush candle! So, good day! I see a cheering breeze springing up, ready to send me through the heavens. I ask no favors, as I have all space to dance in, and the wind to drive my chariot through the heavens. So, good day! —hoping next time to find you more gracious in your demeanor.

SUNBEAM.

Go, plaything of the hour! It is easy to look you through, and see you are like a shallow stream!—a mere inflated emptiness!—

a mere tassel on the robe of day!—mere
flounces on space!—fringes of the heavens!
Go; or, gathering up my fiercest fires, I'll
dispel you, scattering you to the winds, or con-
centrating you into filmy masses, dash you
headlong to earth! Then, robing in ethereal
blue, show all my state to man, without a blot
on my fair escutcheon.

CLOUD.

Indeed! How grand you are, how proud,
when you are dressed in ethereal blue! It is
well; for seldom do I allow you to robe yourself thus. So make much of your state, since
you so seldom can keep it up, for my films are
even mightier than your fierceness; and, being
light and airy, soon surround you in misty
lights and obscure vision. But I disdain to
speak longer. Day-day! I'm off on the
winds; and what a glorious sail on the airy
billows!

SUNBEAM.

A good riddance to such a pest! When you are gone, I can keep up state without a rival; and for a time think I alone am king of the heavens! Good day! and I would that you might stay away forever!

MORAL.—Each is useful in his sphere,—the lowly as well as the great.

THE SEASONS.

A DISPUTE, AND AN APPEAL TO THE YEAR TO DECIDE THEIR MERITS.

PRING, robed in dazzling emerald, garlanded with blossoms and decked with golden and crimson buds, and heralded with soft, sweet-perfumed zephyrs, first comes riding in the lists, wreathed in smiles and joyous in her youth and budding beauty, her cheek all aglow, and musical with many-voiced birds, the twinkle of many rills, and the chirrup of all Creation.

She stood tip-toe, in glowing youth, as if a

sylph of joy, her light bound airy as a star in space.

With conscious pride, and head erect, thus she glowingly expatiated on her charms:—

I am the seed-time of earth! All Nature I now adorn with a million leaflets! I crown the twigs and branches of all Creation with emerald wreathings; and my balmy airs melt ice-bound WINTER, and drive him—hard, and stern, and terrible—into oblivion.

I carpet earth with green bowers, and lace the forests with their crowns of beauty. I hang garlands on Nature's brow, and deck the hoary rocks with vines and creepers. I mantle the old towers in their picturesque loveliness; and make of the cold, bare, uninviting earth, a bower of beauty.

I labyrinth the undergrowth in a maze of tangled emerald, till Nature, in her perfumes, her gay robings, her spangled dresses, stands an unrivalled queen of loveliness.

Behold, how I sport in the April showers, and frolic in dancing merriment, as the big drops come bounding down in their free glory.

I loosen the watercourses that come dashing down in a yeast of foam, waltzing to the music of shivering spray. I invite the spirit of all things to gem my bosom with their seed harvest; and fan them into growth with the sunbeams, which I draw from heaven.

Thus speaking, she stopped, and drew aside, and look!

Who comes clothed in sunbeams, dazzling in raiment, with burning blushes quivering in her cheeks?—with eyes of radiant fire, and mien like a sun-god wrapped in his mantle of flame?

Who is this that rears her fire-steed defiantly, and, leaping to earth, stands in the throng like a salamander of flame?

Who is this beauty, rainbow-gemmed, and

glowing like a new-fledged goddess from the stars? See how the air around her is redolent of perfumes! How the roses hang in garlands around her form! She stands, exultant in her flushed youth, crowned with flowers,— with a high and lofty mien, a very fire-goddess of heaven!

It is SUMMER, in the glory of her prime, Queen of Flowers and of Light, towering in the perfection of growth, full and rounded with the matured beauty of all things.

She stepped forth, and, with lofty mien and voice of high command, thus spoke:—

The thunders and lightnings are handmaids in my train! The clouds do my bidding; and all the artillery of heaven plays its music around me in the fiery showers.

All earth leaps to my warm embrace in love and joy! The harvests ripen beneath my eye! All fruits gain luster, and ripen in beauty! The flowers spring forth, arrayed in loveliness! All hues heighten, and grow dazzling with my touch!

Nature, so coy and young in Spring, with my fiery beams grows to perfect maturity. I am dazzling in fiery light. I am grand and majestic in my lofty nature. I stand crowned with the riches of the universe.

The splendor of profusion is mine, and the luxury of all things abounds; and earth is one garland of emerald and flowers. All unsightly objects I clothe in festoons beautiful.

I awake the energies of man, and earth resounds to the hum of labor. Man gathers from my bosom the luxury of a world. I dry up the stagnant marshes. I drive away colds and rheumatism. I breathe into the weak, and worn, and ailing, my sunbeams, that, like vivifying fire, stir up the stagnant blood; and beneath my banner all life leaps to its fullest enjoyment.

The sportive bathers now leap into the

stream; and the soft, balmy shades of evening, invite all the world to wander forth and enjoy the night.

The luxury of breathing the balmy sweetness of my fragrant breath is indeed an exquisite delight. A haze of loveliness floats around me, as I wander forth.

All Nature becomes supple and elastic at my touch. I unbend the muscles and the nerves, and the earth leaps to sportive life.

The new-mown hay now sends forth its perfume; and the world's staff of life, the golden-shafted wheat, is now gathered from my bosom.

Thus speaking, she mounted her steed of fire, and, with a whirlwind of sparkles glittering around her, she disappeared.

Look! Who is this rainbow-gemmed harlequin of Time, with Nature's cashmere mantle thrown around him, in gorgeous hues, decking his solemn, stately form? A soft dirge, melancholy and sad, wails in the air, as with slow and majestic pace he moves as if loath to leave the earth to stern Winter's command, who will soon usurp his throne, and leave him lost in oblivion.

A mournful beauty hovers over him, a wild scene of enchanting hues blend all things in an indescribable loveliness, almost intoxicating to the eye.

It is AUTUMN, the year's third child of wonder. He arose in all his dolphin hues, a very changeling of light and shade,—now gold, now brown, now purple, now crimson, and now of russet hue.

AUTUMN thus spoke:—

I own I am not fierce and high-spirited of mien like my sister SUMMER, just passed away and gone; but I hold the stately corn and the golden grain in the hollow of my hand. I carry in my bosom the succulent potato, which God designed as the food for millions.

The royal purple buckwheat I now ripen for the use of man.

I temper to man's touch the fierce heats, that, like scorching thunderbolts, have struck him down to death. I give him ease in the mellow breath I blow around him, and gently lead him step by step, in graduated heat and cold, to icy Winter's arms.

I break the spell of Winter's tyranny by being forewarned of his approach. I give rest to the jaded energy of man; and before I tear away the curtain that hides the bare earth, with its frost-king of sleet, hail, and snow, I catch one stray beam of Summer, and almost make him believe it is Spring again. This Indian Summer lull intoxicates him with pleasure, and leaves him balmy with delight. This narcotic dream Nature receives from me, before all the winds of heaven run riot in the mad Winter's rage, dancing whirligigs in its naked fury.

From my veins flows the delicious cider; and from my bosom the store of nuts is gathered to enjoy around the Winter's fires. Now the game and fish are caught for man's feastings.

I give to the tired earth rest; and receive within my bosom the seed-wheat to replenish the earth.

I prepare the couch for the Winter's rest; and I strip Nature of her million leaflets, and unloosen the juices of the trees, and vines, and shrubs, and flowers, that they may sink beneath the earth, away from the hard frosts and the sudden changes which blast the trees and branches exposed to view, to sleep and rest till Spring renews their life, and power, and usefulness.

All earth becomes naked at my touch, that the Winter's howling may not destroy the too heavily laden branches, which, if crowned with leaves, would break beneath the piling masses of snow and ice.

I smother the outward life of all things, which is only their sleep and dreams.

Thus speaking, she fell into the lap of WIN-TER, and was lost to view.

WINTER then arose, and, with the voice of a hurricane, a terrible war-whoop that resounded on the blast, and with furious riding and vaultings and great uprearings, danced a whirligig around.

As he spoke, his face became rigid as marble, his mien like an iceberg, his eye seemed dewy with snowflakes, his face flushed red, and his voice thick with storms, his beard hung with icicles, and his matted locks stiff with cold.

I seem callous, hard, and terrible! I prick mankind like a million needle-points; I sting their fingers and toes; I bite their noses; I make their teeth chatter, and their forms shiver, at my touch; I smother the sun-god in my mantle of ice; I steal his fire, and temper it with my chill breath.

Yet I have my use, and good, and glory. The air becomes pure and resuscitating. I give rest to the husbandman; I build the cheery fire at the household hearth; I give the long nights for rest to man's jaded mind and body; I shorten the day, that his work may be less; I build up the beautiful snowflakes, and then hurrah for the bounding sleigh, the merry bells, the dashing steeds, and away like the wind!

Look at the diamond jewels I scatter everywhere! Look at earth's mirrors of ice, a very sheen of polished beauty!

I furnish the people with ice for their luscious creams and friendly gatherings. I supply the heats of Summer with cool, refreshing drinks; and pile up a storehouse of ice for wonderful use — to preserve all things in Summer's heats.

All Nature now becomes like a rock-bound coast. It is her lethargy to renew again, in sweeter growth, all things.

In this skeleton beauty, in this bold grandeur all around, there is a wierd delight, showing all things in their true shape, and Nature becomes a picturesque outline and tracery; and hued in the twilight, often looks like golden and crimson spires floating in a shadowy light.

Nature's nerves I strengthen with the tonic *cold;* and I brace up the muscles, give rigidity to the bones, which were relaxed in the fierce heats of Summer.

I am the earth's physician, with my wormwood touch, that builds up the tissues and layers the frames of men and animals with fat. I renew them in my frozen reign, so that they may have new life and strength to fight another year against all the changes of the elements.

I give variety to the year, so that an eternal

sameness may not make man blase with too many sweets and soft delights.

God's wise providence makes Winter as a school of trial to harden us, to steel our nerves, and also as a source of pleasure and delight. Conviviality now reigns, and pleasure lets loose its thousand fancies for the sport of man.

There is a wild fascination in my reign, that many even prefer me to soft Summer's sway.

Though my grip is rigid as iron, and I lock Nature stiff and fast in my embrace, yet it is the grip of love, and usefulness, and power; and, in a million ways, benefits man. I yield not to any of the seasons in my reverence for God, as an agent to do His will.

The YEAR recalled her children, and thus addressed them:—

My darlings, don't dispute! Each and all, in God's wise design, have their duties and their merits. He appointed me to superintend your power, and glory, and beauty, and use-fulness.

Each of you is dear to me, and I could not choose between you; for each has a glory of its own,—apart, distinct, yet together forming a transcendent whole; and the duties of each so merge into one another, that one is as necessary to the year as the other, showing Divine knowledge and the goodness and great-ness of the Creator and His care and blessing for man,—giving every climate, every change of heat and cold, every fruit, and food for bird, insect, animal, and vegetable life, and every soil to suit their growth. Air for some, water for some, earth for some, apportioned beautifully for their wants and uses, joys, life, and procreation.

The earth appears a desolate waste. Its icy heart seems barren and inert. All things look like death. Nakedness robes the bosom of Creation. Yet thou, my first-born child, oh

SPRING! with thy eye of light, thy sunny smile, bursts forth to robe the earth anew in a glowing splendor of emerald, with forms of exquisite chiselings clothing the desolate twigs and branches.

With thy soft touch thou charmest the icebound streams, torrents, rivers, lakes, and watercourses, till they dance in glee, and rush on with sportive freedom, making music as they go along.

The hard earth, rock-bound in Winter's icy arms, thou meltest into softness; and the tiny seeds of herb, flower, plant, and vine, thou coaxeth up from earth, and, smiling on them with thy genial face, they exultingly peep forth, living gems of beauty, in their first robings, like light fleeces of emerald down.

This bridal fleece of the new year is surpassingly beautiful; and, quivering in the sunbeams, forms Nature's fairy palace, an exquisite wonder to the strange contrast of your stern brother WINTER, being almost a mockery of his power and sway.

Labor, sluggish and inert, now puts forth new energy; and all mankind, and beast, and bird, and insect, now herald new life, and joy, and promise. Nature smiles as at a new birth, and exultingly claps her hands in glee.

There is a freedom in all things,—an awakening, a revival; and strains delicious as those in heaven fill the earth in homage and in joy for this new-born life! And thou, my child, oh SUMMER! continuest the glad work; and, like twins of toil, perfect this beauty and this growth, till the luxury of Summer fills all earth with the storehouse of plenty and promise.

Thou, oh SUMMER, art a marvel of beauty; and thy twilights and thy moonlights are exquisite in their loveliness.

Thou openest the pores of all things to take

in the warm sunbeams; and earth, refreshed, renews her strength, beauty, and usefulness.

The flowers crown thee Queen! The jeweled wheat hangs pendant in thy ears, luscious life of vegetable and fruit fills thy garners, and all earth rejoices at thy profusion.

The lame, the sick, the weak, now bask in thy sunny smile, and drink in thy soft air. The earth perspires, and throws off her weakness, and receives a new cuticle fresh as the morning. The fields resound with the hum of labor, and cheery brightness attends upon thy footsteps. Thou art, indeed, like a young bride in her gayest robes, lighted up with her sweetest smile; or, rather, like a young matron zoned with a pair of cherubs, sweet prattlers of innocence and love.

And thou, gentle AUTUMN, with thy sad and sober mien, beguiling time with thy fantastic paintings, thou hast thy post of duty, as noble, as great, as thy twin sister's gone before.

The world loves thy sway equally as well; for there are hours in thy realms to man of most exquisite witchery, as if earth lay under a holy spell,—days of transcendent loveliness, with such balmy airs as almost makes us believe we are in heaven.

O'er WINTER's icy form thou hurlest thy prismatic robe, veiling his approach in the wild frolic of thy hues, and softening his mien for a while in thy Indian Summer opiate.

In those hours of dreamy delight, what visions come, as if from the regions of the blest? Thou art Nature's apology for the Winter's hardness, a softener of his rude behavior, a warning of his near approach.

Thou art a sweet spangled herald, proclaiming his inexorable march,—a stay between fierce Summer and iron-hearted Winter. Thou relaxest Summer's heat and tempereth fierce Winter's power. Thou givest the world time to prepare the fight against the Frost King, with his hail, ice, and snow; and in thy duties we crown thee equal to the rest.

And thou, last child of my soul, stern inexorable Winter, the terror of the earth to those who understand thee not, but to him who does, a strange fierce delight. Man exults in thy wild storms: they mettle his bounding blood, and send high resolve to endure and fight thy strange charms.

There is a sublime grandeur in facing unshrinking the fierce cold, to stand before the storm, to make Nature's icy heart melt before man's high resolve or his genius, by counteracting by art his deadly touch, deadly only in neglect. In care, Winter becomes a great ever-changing delight.

It is full of magic power to tone our system, and brace our nerves and muscles. It is meant for good, if we wisely understand God's plan on earth.

Thy hall of ice, oh Winter!—thy jewels,

thy frost-work lacings, thy icy embroidery, thy tassels of snow, thy feathery flounces, thy ermine fleeces,—artistically and picturesquely woven and interwoven on tree, shrub, rock, and mount,—is like a fairy palace of wonder, so light, and bright, and delicate, as almost to be beyond belief. I have seen thee so marvelously beautiful, as if all heaven's mines were opened, and it rained down jewels, gems so unique and strange as to be indescribable, and must be seen to be understood,—webs of lace spun upon the ground, queer tracery everywhere, and fantastic lacings, as if conceived in fairyland.

Thy halls, oh WINTER, are filled with trophies that can match the world.

Thy royal ermine is a canopy for the gods; and thy air is filled with floating spirits that whisper a dirge-like dream, beautiful as the dying echoes of the spirit-worlds on high.

When all things on earth are filled with thy

floating down, the spirit of purity and loveliness hovers o'er the world, as if God had sent Heaven's dove-pinions to mantle earth with the love, the sweetness, the gentleness, of the skies.

I am proud of my wonderful quartette; and challenge the universe to outmatch their state, and beauty, use and power.

My children, like the hues of the rainbow, which so mingle into each other as scarcely to show each dividing color, so beautifully blended are all hues,—so you encroach on each other's domain so usefully and so properly as to prop each other, and alone each would be nought; but together you carry on all life, activity, and beauty, food and drink, for millions, and paint scenes of indescribable loveliness.

Ye are all artists of light and shade, gods of cold and heat, and ye make of earth an ever-changing kaleidoscope, whose glasses were made in heaven, hues born of celestial dyes, and forms as varied as the phases of the soul of the Great Spirit.

MORAL.—A variety of occupations and powers, mingling harmoniously together, add greatly to their profit and pleasure.